The Merman - Boo

Gabriel Braven is destined for a ɡ. ... .. ., ... it.

His parents had a storybook romance … until a freak ocean storm robbed them of their lives and left him alone to be raised by his grandmother. With their deaths, Gabriel's adoration for the sea turned to fear, and his belief in happy-ever-afters turned to dust. Gabriel vowed to never set foot in the ocean again and to never believe in love.

Gabriel kept that promise until after his junior year of college, when he and his best friend Corey return to the ocean-side town where he lost his parents in order to help his grandmother. Gabriel's bitter fear of the water has only grown, along with his belief that it is his destiny to be forever alone.

Corey is determined to prove Gabriel wrong. It is his mission that summer for Gabriel to find love on the beach … and maybe do some swimming, too. Gabriel will settle for simply not reliving his parents' deaths every time he hears the rush and shush of the waves.

Both may get their wish as Gabriel discovers the hidden past of the Bravens and the sea sends *someone amazing* to his aid.

THE MERMAN

BOOK 1: TRANSFORMATION
A RAYTHE REIGN NOVEL
Based on the novel The Sea by X. Aratare

Story by X. Aratare

Cover Art by Mathia Arkoniel

If you would like to see more of Raythe Reign Publishing, Inc.'s offerings please go to:

www.RaytheReign.com

Use Coupon Code 92DDC246EC
and pay only 1 Penny for a Month!

PUBLISHING

THE MERMAN

BOOK 1 - TRANSFORMATION

X. ARATARE
STORY

MATHIA ARKONIEL
COVER ART

Chapter 1

LIGHTS IN THE DEEP

 *welve years ago ...*

"We're going sailing today, right?" Nine-year-old Gabriel Braven couldn't quite keep the slightest plea from his voice as he spoke to his parents. The need to get out on the water when they went to his grandmother's cottage was always strong, but on this visit it was almost overwhelming.

Something is going to happen. Something amazing. Those two thoughts chased each other through his head like rambunctious

6

squirrels. There was no concrete reason for feeling this way. He just felt it, like he felt the warmth of the sun shining through the kitchen windows in his grandmother's cottage.

His mother and father exchanged smiles over the tops of their coffee cups. His father John Braven reached over and ruffled Gabriel's black hair. He was handsome and strong with deeply tanned limbs even though summer had just begun.

"Eager to get out on the water, Gabriel?" he asked.

"Totally!" Gabriel replied and nodded, a smile stretching from ear to ear. He could hear the surf through the open back door that led out onto his grandmother's porch. The ocean was just fifty feet away. It called to him like a siren song.

His family came to Ocean Side every summer to stay with his grandmother and sail the boat that his father kept there. Her cottage sat on an isolated point, surrounded on three sides by the sea. Every moment Gabriel could, he spent out on the water or in it. The sea was in his blood.

"I don't know, Gabriel. We had a long drive yesterday. Maybe we should just stay on land for now and rest. Will my water baby wither away if we don't sail?" His mother Kathleen's green eyes sparkled as she teased him.

"Not a *baby*, Mom." He scrapped his fork through his scrambled eggs. They were as yellow and bright as the sunny kitchen. He gazed out the back door, almost as if he were considering making a run for it. He just had to get out on the boat today. Going in the water near the beach was good, but he knew he had to feel deep water beneath him. He wouldn't feel *right* without it.

"Don't tease him any more, you two. He's been practically quivering to get on the boat since you got here yesterday," his grandmother Grace said from her spot in front of the sink. She was already cleaning the dishes even though breakfast had just ended. Gabriel knew that she hated being idle and was always cleaning, cooking or working on something. She was running for councilwoman of Ocean Side, and he was sure she would win and then clean up the town, too.

"He's nine. He quivers at lots of things." John winked at his son.

"You're forty-two and you're just the same," Grace said with a smile. "What's your excuse?"

His father flushed and lowered his head with a rueful smile on his lips. "You're right, Mom. I'm dying to get out there myself. Let's go."

A rush of relief went through Gabriel. *Something is going to happen. Something amazing.*

"I already packed a cooler with sandwiches and drinks. All we have to do is grab it off the back porch," Kathleen said. "C'mon, kiddo."

"You mean you were planning on us going out all along?" Gabriel let out a shocked laugh.

His mother tipped back her head and laughed. "And have you and your father sulking all day if we didn't? I think not."

"You're the best, Mom!"

"I try." Her chair scraped across the floor as she stood up.

"Have fun. I'll be sure to have a big dinner ready for my sailors when you come back," Grace called.

Gabriel launched himself to his feet and ran out onto the back porch. The scent of salt and the sound of gulls calling to one another as they wheeled overhead enveloped him. The breeze off the ocean was cool, which was a relief from the superheated air. Even though it was only 10 a.m., he already knew the day was going to be blisteringly hot.

"Not a cloud in the sky," his father said as he stepped out onto the porch beside Gabriel. "Perfect sailing weather."

"We're going to go out real far today, right, Dad?" Gabriel asked. Now that he was actually looking at the ocean, it felt like there was a string attached to the center of his chest and the other end was being held by an invisible hand in the depths of the ocean.

Something is going to happen. Something amazing.

"Real far. You pick the direction and we'll take off for it." His father squeezed his shoulder.

"I've already decided where we're going to go," Gabriel said softly.

"Really?" His father's brow furrowed.

Gabriel found himself lifting one hand up. The string seemed to move from his chest to the tip of his pointer finger. His hand wavered in the air before it moved a few degrees off center. "There. That's where we have to go."

The place he was pointing to looked no different from where they were standing than anywhere else on the horizon, but Gabriel *knew* that was where they had to go. That's where the *something* was. He nodded to himself.

"Okay, kiddo. We'll go *there*. Wherever there is!" His father laughed.

Gabriel didn't join in the laughter. He felt strangely calm now that it had been decided and there was nothing left to get in the way.

"Is there something you see out there, Gabriel?" His mother noticed his fixed stare at the special place.

"I don't know. I just feel ..." He paused. "I feel like we'll *find* something there. Something important."

Something amazing.

His mother surveyed the sky. "The radio is reporting bad weather brewing, but it certainly doesn't look like it. We should stay close to shore though, just in case."

"No!" The word burst from Gabriel's lips before he could help himself.

His mother's green eyes widened. "Honey?"

"Sorry, Mom. Dad said I got to pick where we go. I already picked the place, and I really, really want to go there, and I know you'll say it's too far!"

"Son, if you talk to your mother that way we won't be going out at all," John warned.

Gabriel swallowed down the sudden panic that flooded him.

"I'm sorry, Mom."

She patted his arm. "I know, honey. If it really means that much to you we'll go. What's a little bad weather?"

John put an arm around her shoulders and kissed her cheek. "When has the weather service been right about anything, Kate? Have you ever seen a more beautiful blue sky?"

"I think Grace is correct that you're just as eager to get on the water as Gabriel is. They could be forecasting a hurricane and you'd want to go out in the boat 'just for a little while.'" She grinned and kissed him back.

"Don't you feel the same?" John asked.

Her gaze swept over to the water. The luminous smile on her face faded slightly. "I love the sea. But I love you two more."

John's expression went serious. "If you're really worried, Kathleen, then we won't go out. We could swim here."

Gabriel's chest seized again. What would he do if they decided not to go? He had the wild idea to try and take the boat out himself or even swim the distance. He had to get out there!

"Can we go out for just a tiny bit? We don't have to stay out that long. Just for an hour or so? And if it looks bad, if even one cloud comes out, we'll go in. Please?" Gabriel wheedled.

His mother relented at his puppy-dog eyes and slight lip wobble. She smiled down at him. "All right, so long as we're all agreed that at the first sign of trouble, we go in. I'm dying to sail as much as you are, Gabriel."

"Thanks, Mom!"

"So easy to make him happy," John said, but he brightened, too.

She kissed him tenderly. "You look pretty happy yourself."

He grinned. "You're the wind beneath my … sails."

She laughed and playfully hit his shoulder. "I'm glad I could make both the men in my life happy."

Gabriel just smiled at his parents and shook his head. It didn't matter if they were doing their lovey-dovey thing. He was going out onto the ocean!

"Get the cooler, Gabriel," John said.

"Got it." Gabriel picked it up with two hands. It was comfortingly heavy, indicating that it was full of sandwiches and sodas.

The three of them then walked down the steps that led from the porch onto the beach. The sailboat was anchored about one hundred feet from shore. They would take the dinghy that his father kept stored under a lean-to near the water to get over to it. His father pulled the dinghy out and flipped it over, then took the cooler from Gabriel and set it securely on the bottom of the boat.

"Get in, Gabriel. You too, Kathleen. I'll push you both out."

Gabriel and his mother scrambled into the dinghy. His father's bronzed arms and calves flexed as he pushed the boat out into the water with ease. Gabriel let out a whoop as soon as he heard the slap of waves against the boat's bottom. His father vaulted into the dinghy and took up the oars. His strokes were powerful and sure as he rowed out to the white-hulled, thirty-eight foot sailboat.

His mother tossed her hair back in the breeze. It hung down to her shoulders and curled becomingly around her face like a bronze wave. His father's gaze was fixed on her as he rowed. She smiled back at him. As much as watching them adore one another caused Gabriel to roll his eyes now, some part of him knew he would want someone to look at him exactly the same way one day in the future.

In the far future.

His father's rowing slowed and then stopped as they reached the stern of the boat, where a steel ladder hung down. "Gabriel, go up and tie us off."

Gabriel grabbed the end of the line that was attached to the front of the dinghy and leaped lightly up the ladder, not needing to catch his balance as the bobbing waves rocked the boat. On water, unlike on land, he was graceful and sure of himself. He tied the dinghy securely to the cleat at the top of the ladder. "All set."

His mother went up next while his father remained below, watching to make sure that his wife safely got to the top.

"Hand me the cooler, John," she said once she reached the last rung.

"It's heavy. Be careful," he warned.

She just smiled at his fussing. The muscles in her arms rippled as she easily took the cooler from him and put it on deck. John came up directly after her. He was grinning even wider than normal as he set foot on the boat. His father always tried to find the brightness in life, but he seemed to shed any concerns he had when he was on the water.

"Let's get that anchor up, Gabriel, and take off," John said.

None too soon, the anchor was stored in the forward compartment and the mainsail was fluttering in the wind. The colorful jib flew next, curling around the boat like an embracing arm. The breeze filled it and the sailcloth billowed and rippled.

Gabriel raced to the bow of the boat. He had always loved riding up and down on the waves as the boat raced through the water, but this time he wanted to be on the bow so that he could feel exactly when they reached the special place. From there, he would be able to see everything. His father took his place behind the wheel while his mother finished putting their cooler down below in the cabin.

"Which direction again, Gabe?" his father called.

Gabriel faced forward. The sea seemed to stretch out before them endlessly. His right arm lifted and unerringly went to a spot that looked indistinguishable from the rest of the horizon. With his father's laughter ringing in his ears at his certainty, the boat began to make its way to Gabriel's chosen spot.

They had been sailing for about an hour when his mother joined Gabriel at the bow. She sat down behind him, spreading her legs to either side so he could snuggle between them and rest his head against her chest. He felt too old to be cuddled, but he loved the smell of her violet-scented perfume, plus they could both hold on to the railing that way, so he allowed it. She kissed his head above his right ear.

"I wish Corey could be here," Gabriel said, meaning Corey Rudman, his best friend. The big curly-haired redhead was always laughing and forcing Gabriel out of his shell. Corey had taken the shy and uncertain Gabriel under his wing when they were just five, and they had been inseparable ever since.

"I know, but his parents already planned a trip for them out West this summer."

"He didn't want to go, though! He wanted to come with *us*," Gabriel said sullenly.

She let out a soft laugh. "Corey wants to be wherever you are, Gabe, and vice versa. That's what being best friends is all about."

"Yeah, I guess. I just know he'd love Grandma and everything."

"Next time we'll bring him along." They sat quietly for a moment before his mother asked, "Have I ever told you about the Mers and their Guardian that are supposed to haunt these waters?"

Gabriel's forehead furrowed. "Mers?"

"*Mermen* and *mermaids*," she whispered conspiratorially.

"Mermen - they're not real!"

"Are you so sure?" she asked, and he could hear the impish smile in her voice.

"Okay, Mom. Tell me about them then," Gabriel challenged.

"Well, anyone who has lived around here any length of time has seen strange things in the water at least once," she said.

"I haven't!"

"There's still time for you yet," she laughed. "But one of the very strangest things that are seen are the Mers. People swear to have glimpsed beautiful naked men and women swimming far out at sea. They only appear on the clearest of days or most moonless of nights," she said.

"And how does the Guardian come into this?"

"They're protected by the Guardian. For you see, if the Mers are ever attacked, the Guardian rises up from the deep to save them," she explained.

"Who would want to hurt them?"

"Their beauty is supposed to drive people mad, to make them

do terrible things that they otherwise wouldn't do," she said.

"And what does the Guardian look like?" Gabriel asked. "I'm guessing it's not beautiful?"

She stroked his hair back from his forehead. "No, it's not. Those who have seen it and survived can only speak of something miles high with tentacles."

Gabriel felt a strange chill go down his spine. "Miles high with tentacles, huh?"

"Yes, that can grab the unwary like … *this*!" She immediately began to tickle his ribs.

"MOM!" Gabriel cried out through his laughter. He squirmed around to face her and began to tickle her back. She collapsed helplessly when he got to her sides and arms. She was red-faced and gasping before he finally relented.

"Ah, enough, enough!" she pleaded.

"That's what you get for telling me about a monster, Mom," he said.

"I suppose so," she said. Her expression went thoughtful. "People really do claim to have seen the Mers. I thought I saw one too, once. Staring at me right back."

"Really? Where, Mom? Around here? What did you do?" Gabriel asked.

She opened her mouth to answer, but then her gaze fixed on something over his shoulder. That was when he heard the crack of lightning. He whipped around. The formerly cloudless horizon had filled with a welling line of black clouds. The slow, silky waves changed to choppy swells. His mother scrambled to her feet and helped him up.

"John!" she cried. Her face had gone chalk white.

"I see it!" he yelled back. His father was already white-knuckling the wheel. "We've got to turn around. Get back to shore *now*."

"Where did the storm come from?" Gabriel crouch-walked back to the stern, holding on to the railing as tightly as he could. The boat had begun to buck up and down. "It was sunny!"

"The ocean can turn on a dime, Gabriel," his mother said. Her expression was grim. She quickly joined his father behind the wheel.

That was when Gabriel felt it. They were at the spot. He wavered where he stood. Something was beneath them. Something far below.

This is where we were meant to come.

His mother's voice, high and tight, broke him out of his reverie. "John, let's get the motor on and the sails down. I'll take over here." She gestured towards the wheel.

His father nodded tightly. He stopped to cup Gabriel's cheek, probably thinking the strange expression on his face was fear. "It's going to be all right, Gabe. Don't worry. We're going to be fine. We'll keep ahead of the storm. I'll get the sails. Why don't you turn the engine on?"

But the storm was already upon them. A line of darkness crossed over the boat. Gabriel watched as the sun was snuffed out. The wind nearly blew him over as he stumbled towards where the controls for the motor were. The line holding the dinghy snapped and the little boat floated several yards away before being swamped by a wave and disappearing below the surface. Lightning crackled above them. Thunder suddenly boomed, and Gabriel felt the vibration in his chest.

His father had untied the line and was winching the jib closed. The muscles in his arms and legs stood out as he used all of his strength against the power of the wind. Gabriel tried turning the key to get the engine to start, but nothing happened.

"Mom, Dad, it's not turning over!"

His father turned to come help him, but his mother waved him off.

"John, get the mainsail down first! Then we can deal with the engine!" Kathleen cried.

The wind was making the mainsail snap violently, and there was now an ominous tilt to the boat. Gabriel had to hang on to one of the cleats to stop from tumbling into the sea.

"Damn!" John jumped up and headed towards the mast.

Gabriel was watching his father with anxious eyes when he glimpsed something huge and black rising up from the ocean in front of them. He heard his mother scream for his father. His father turned and saw the rogue wave. There was nothing they could do. They couldn't get out of the way. His father didn't even have time to get back to them. The massive wave blotted out Gabriel's ability to think. And then his father, his mother, and the boat were all gone.

He was in the water.

It was amazingly quiet underneath the waves. The thunder was muted. The lightning that ripped across the sky wasn't as bright. Everything was peaceful. Calm. Gabriel could see the boat floating above him, only it wasn't quite right. The mast was snapped in the middle, hanging on by a few thin strands of fiberglass. It should have been pointing at the sky, but was now straining towards the bottom of the ocean. The boat had capsized. For one moment, he thought of just staying where he was. It felt so much safer under the water. But then his lungs began to ache. He had to surface. He had to face the storm.

He swam towards the lightning-streaked sky. Gasping as he broke the surface, Gabriel frantically looked around for his parents. His eyes stung from the salt water. He blinked them clear. Where were his mother and father? He grabbed hold of the boat's barnacle-encrusted bottom. The sharp barnacles sliced through his palms, but his blood was quickly washed away by the sea. Lightning crackled across the sky. Another round of thunder reverberated in his chest.

"MOM! DAD!"

His head was again pushed beneath the ocean's surface by another wave, not as big as the one that had capsized the boat, but powerful all the same. His eyes popped open underwater. He looked around him trying to see his parents' bodies in the dimness. He thought he saw a flash of white, maybe an arm or a leg, about twenty feet away. And there was something else, something deep below him.

Lights? A submarine? No, it's too big. Many colors, not just white. So deep below …

The lights were red and blue and green and yellow and purple. They were distant, yet for some reason he felt the insane urge to try and swim down to them. But his lungs were already burning again. Strangely, so were his sides. They burned and itched. Gabriel raced to the surface for air. He gulped down oxygen greedily. The burning sensation in his lungs eased, but his sides still felt odd.

He turned to face where he had seen the flash of a limb. However, the slate gray sea showed nothing but foaming, storm-churned water.

"MOM! DAD! Where are you?" Gabriel's voice was whipped back to him by the wind.

That was when he caught sight of his mother. She was on the opposite side of the boat. Her hair was plastered to her face like seaweed and her green eyes were so wide they swallowed everything else.

"Gabe! Oh, my God! Hold on to the boat! Don't let go!" she cried.

Air trapped in the cabin must have been keeping the boat afloat. Pelting rain suddenly started coming down on them in torrents. The drops stung like acid on the backs of his hands as he stretched them over the bottom of the boat. Barnacles cut into the soft inner skin of his arms.

"Where's Dad?" he shouted at her. He couldn't see his strong, handsome father anywhere.

His mother's head swiveled around. A look of panic flooded her features.

"John?" she cried out. "JOHN?"

But no one responded.

The waves lashed them from all sides. Gabriel's grip on the boat was slipping, but he doggedly held on. A large wave lifted the boat, letting them see more clearly all around them. That was when he caught sight of his father.

"There! There he is, Mom!" Gabriel pointed towards his father. His father's body was bobbing up and down on the waves. He didn't appear to be moving on his own. "I'll go get him!"

"No, Gabriel! Stay here!" she ordered. "I'm going to get your father. And then we'll swim back to you. We'll come back to you."

"But—"

"NO!" She looked wild then. "Gabriel, stay with the boat. No matter what, you stay with the boat!"

She stared at him until he nodded his agreement. Every part of him was fighting against it.

"I love you, Gabriel." She said the words as if she were trying to imprint them on him.

"I love you, too, Mom." His voice sounded hollow.

She cast one last look at him and then she let go of the boat and swam out after his father. He watched as she swam with sure and steady strokes towards him even against the wildness of the sea. She would get to his father. She would swim them both back to the boat. Then they would all figure out a way to get back to shore. It would be all right. Everything would be all right.

Sea spray lifted off of the ocean's surface and splashed into his eyes. He lost sight of his mother and father, but when his vision cleared he saw something else. It was another rogue wave. A wall of black water, ten times his height, was bearing down towards him. The wave was already breaking at the top. White foam frothed at the tip as the wave began to collapse.

His hands slid away from the boat's slowly sinking bottom. The wave smashed down on top of him, sending him spiraling into the depths, far too deep to make it back to the surface before his lungs gave out. He barely was able to escape being snagged by the boat on its way down to the ocean's distant floor.

He looked around for his parents, but there was nothing left but water and the lights. His parents were gone and he knew that they were dead. He felt it inside of him, and the grief was too huge to grasp. He looked up and couldn't see the surface. He tried to take a few strokes upwards, but his lungs were already screaming for air and his arms and legs felt leaden. His sides were burning like a knife was being punched through his skin again and again.

I'm drowning, he thought, and was surprised at how numb he was to that fact.

Black spots began to dance before his eyes. In a moment his mouth was going to open, and he was going to try and draw in air that wasn't there whether he wanted it to happen or not. Water was going to rush past his lips and flood his lungs. He would spasm and there would be pain and panic. It had already happened to his parents. It would happen to him.

The lights below him dimmed slightly, as if something impossibly large had passed in front of them. In what he thought would be his last conscious moment, he looked down once more. He thought he saw something reaching up towards him. It was long and sinuous. He knew he must be hallucinating, because what caught ahold of him, what began to draw him to the surface and from there towards shore, appeared to be a gigantic tentacle. The tentacle was attached to something miles high swimming below him in the ocean's murky depths.

Much later, when he awoke alone on the beach next to the old Morse place, a mile and a half from his grandmother's cottage and somehow still alive, he would tell himself that monsters didn't exist. Like Mers and their Guardian, such things were not real. But part of him would know the truth even as he clung to the lie.

Chapter 2

THRUM

*T*he present ...

Twenty-one year old Gabriel Braven looked around his empty college dorm room to make sure that he and Corey had packed everything. After tonight's end of the school year party, they wouldn't be in any state in the morning to finish up. Hopefully his grandmother wouldn't mind if they were just a little hung over when they made it to her place. They were going to spend the entire summer with her, so one day of being a little worse for wear shouldn't be that bad.

The room was stripped bare. It was hard to believe it had been a clothes-strewn, empty pizza box pit just a few days ago when he and Corey had been cramming for their junior year finals. But now finals were done. School was over for the year and summer stretched before him like a golden road. Only he wasn't feeling as happy about it as he should.

His grandmother had moved back to Ocean Side. He wasn't upset or angry with her for going back to the sea. He understood why. He was only home a few months a year now, and soon even that would end as he and Corey took off on their own. Why should she have to keep living in an inland apartment instead of the cottage by the ocean where Bravens had lived for centuries? As she neared retirement she needed to conserve money. The cottage was already paid for. The apartment was rented. He couldn't expect her to accommodate him more than she already had.

He and Corey were planning on spending the entire summer with her at the cottage helping to sort out hundreds of years of Braven family history that was stored in the cottage's basement and attic. It would be the first time he had been back there since his parents' deaths. But he could handle it. He was a grown man. He could face down his fear of the ocean. He had to.

"Feeling nostalgic?" Corey asked as he threw one pudgy arm around Gabriel's broad shoulders. "We'll be in an apartment next year. Far better than our little rat hole here, though this rat hole has been good to us for three years."

"Our rat hole. Our dear, sweet rat hole," Gabriel deadpanned.

"Now *I'm* feeling nostalgic." Corey sniffed dramatically.

Gabriel playfully jabbed his elbow into Corey's ample side. He and Corey had grown up to be as different in character as they were in body type. Gabriel was tall and lean, with deep blue eyes and black hair. He had a swimmer's build even though he now loathed the water, and a perpetual golden tan despite the fact that he spent little time outdoors anymore. Corey's nickname was Young Santa Claus. He was built like the jolly man, stout with a large belly that shook when he laughed. Instead of snow white hair, though, he had a bright red curly mane and a matching beard.

"There are some things I won't miss, though," Gabriel said. "For example, I was checking to see if your toothpaste patch job was holding up."

"It's a thing of beauty, isn't it?"

Corey gestured towards the section of wall where a poster had once hung. When they had tried to take down the hook that held the poster up a large section of wall plaster had come down with it. Corey had used a whole tube of white toothpaste as filler to patch it up. He had then "aged" it with a tea wash so the patch looked the same as the rest of the yellowing wall.

"Yeah, until someone wonders where that minty fresh smell is coming from when they hammer in a nail," Gabriel laughed.

Corey let out a rueful sigh. "Nothing's perfect, is it?"

"No, I guess not." Gabriel glanced at his watch. "We should head over to the party, yeah?"

"Are you sure you're feeling up to it?"

"I'm good. Seriously."

Gabriel shook his head at his friend's mother-henning. He had been sick on and off all year. Nothing specific, just tired, flu-ish, and achy. He was always dehydrated, spending hours in the shower when his skin felt too tight. The campus doctors had found nothing wrong with him, though his blood work had seemed off somehow. They thought it was a problem with the lab and not him. He was going to see a new doctor when he went to Ocean Side.

"Hmmm, well if that changes, you let me know," Corey said.

"Yes, Dr. Corey."

"I don't think you salute doctors. But I'll take it. Okay, come on, let's go."

Corey led the way out of the dorm room, which seemed smaller and emptier than Gabriel remembered it ever being. Their van was parked near the dorm's back door. It was loaded with all of their things, and sat lower to the ground than usual.

"Better watch out for speed bumps, Corey, otherwise you'll take out the whole exhaust system."

"The old girl is sort of dragging her belly on the ground, isn't she? But it'll be okay. She's a trooper. Hasn't let us down yet."

Corey leaped up into the driver's seat and the van sank another inch. Gabriel did the same on the passenger side, but more gingerly. The last thing they needed was for the van to break down now.

Though that would mean a delay in going to Ocean Side. But we have to go sooner or later. Need to just do this. Gabriel wiped his suddenly damp palms on the front of his jeans.

"So … I hear that Mark is going to be at the party tonight," Corey said too casually after they had been driving for a few minutes. His bright brown eyes skittered from the road to Gabriel then back again. Mark was one of the many potential boyfriends that Corey had picked out for him.

Gabriel groaned softly. "I thought I would be safe from your matchmaking tonight."

"You are never safe from the hand of love."

Gabriel swung around to face Corey full-on, sputtering, "Hand of love? You're joking."

"You are fated to find a great love, Gabe. You'll see," Corey said with a smile.

"Well, it's not fated to happen tonight. It's the end of the year and I won't be seeing Mark or anyone else from school except you for three months. Sort of pointless to start a relationship now when it won't even last twenty-four hours."

"It'll give you a head start on next year." Corey wagged his finger in Gabriel's face. "It's never too early to start developing a relationship."

Gabriel shook his head. "I'm a confirmed bachelor, Corey."

"At twenty-one?"

"Yes, at twenty-one. When you're married with ten red-haired children as nuts as you, I'll be the eccentric single uncle who brings them too many presents and tells them stories about your crazy days."

"Speaking of stories, *Swimmers in the Deep* has half the guys and gals on campus swooning over you, and here you are swearing off the entire human race for love!"

Corey was talking about a story Gabriel had written that had gotten published in the school's fiction journal. He had written it after finding out about his grandmother's move back to the cottage. He couldn't fight off the feelings that had risen up within him with twelve-mile runs and endless studying. He had started writing as an outlet, thinking he would tell a story about his parents and purge himself of some of his grief and fear, but that wasn't what came when he wrote. Instead, he had written about the myth of the Mers that his mother had told him about.

In his story, a man glimpsed one of the Mers in the sea and could not forget him. The love that ignited within the human man was unquenchable. One single glimpse of that beautiful swimmer and he had been lost forever. Gabriel had ended the story with the man walking into the sea, thinking he would either drown or the Mer would reappear and save him. Either way the agony of loving the Mer and not knowing whether such love was real would be over. Gabriel had left it for the readers to decide what happened.

After he finished it, he had sent it in on a whim to the journal, sure that it wouldn't be published. On the off chance that it was accepted, he was still safe because nobody read the fiction journal anyways. But it had been published, and somehow, inexplicably, it had gone viral. It seemed like everyone had read it. His gay love story had become an impossible, improbable hit. People actually sought him out to talk about it, which still flummoxed him to no end. But after being accosted for the hundredth time, he had figured out *why* the story had resonated with so many people.

Now, sitting in the van, Gabriel tried to explain that "why" to Corey. "Love is nothing compared to longing."

"Okay, what the heck does that mean?"

Gabriel took in a deep breath. "I write with longing and about longing. I think it reflects reality for a lot of people. None of us is going to find someone like the Mer in real life. A love so perfect like that is … rare."

An image of his mother and father looking at one another that last day on the boat juxtaposed with his mother's determined expression as she swam out to her unconscious husband flashed in front of his mind's eye.

So rare it can't survive.

"So you're finally admitting then that you *do* want a relationship? You're even *longing* for one, but you're not going to do anything to find it?" Corey's forehead puckered as he obviously tried to reconcile the idea of Gabriel both wanting and not wanting a relationship at the same time.

"Maybe I like longing for a relationship more than having an actual relationship," Gabriel admitted. "It definitely works for writing."

"I would rather see you in a relationship than on the bestseller list."

"I'm not sure yet about either thing, Corey. It's odd being *known*," Gabriel admitted. "I never thought anyone would read that story, let alone want to talk to me about it."

"That's why you are afraid of relationships! You don't want anyone to know you, and that's what a relationship is all about. But Cupid is planning a love trap for you this summer," Corey said with a happy nod.

"Love trap? Cupid? Oh boy, you're really scaring me now!" Gabriel tipped back his head and laughed.

Corey pulled at his beard. "Do not be afraid, young padawan. I shall save you from the forces of aloneness."

"Now I'm *absolutely* terrified."

Gabriel looked over into his best friend's cherubic face and couldn't help but smile. Corey had a good heart. He would never be able to understand Gabriel's intense solitary nature. It had only been Corey's gentle, but insistent desire to be Gabriel's friend that had broken through the boy's shell all those years ago. Only around family had Gabriel ever been fully at ease, and Corey had become family.

But the idea of letting anyone else in? No thanks.

"Looks like they started the party without us," Corey suddenly said and pointed out the windshield toward a house.

Gabriel could already see the glow of a huge bonfire out back on the beach. There were people everywhere. Red and white plastic cups already littered the street and drunken laughter spilled out from dozens of mouths.

"I don't think we're going to find parking here," Gabriel muttered.

"Oh, ye of little faith! Watch the magic happen."

Corey drew the van over to the side of the road and parked in a space that didn't look big enough to hold them, but somehow his best friend made it happen. He didn't even tap the other cars he parked between. He turned off the van. The tick of the engine was muted by the sound of waves. Gabriel tensed. He realized that he was white-knuckling the strap of the seat belt.

"As a man who hates the water, why did you choose a school in an ocean front city again?" Corey asked.

"Just a masochist, I guess."

"I knew you had kinky tendencies, Gabe." Again came the wagging finger.

The truth was that he had thought about going to school in the middle of the country, far away from large bodies of water, but the idea had terrified him even more than living next to the sea ever could. Even though he kept mostly to campus and away from the water, he still *knew* it was there and he needed that, despite the fact he couldn't explain it to himself or anyone else. Going to this party right on the beach would be the closest he had come to the ocean since going to school. But both he and Corey had thought it would be good preparation for going to Ocean Side.

Corey looked down at the seat belt that Gabriel was holding in a death grip. "You have to undo that if you're going to get out of the car."

"Yeah, right, completely."

Gabriel unhooked his seat belt with shaking hands and opened the van's door. He tried to breathe. The blaring rock music didn't block out the sound of the waves, nor was it dimmed by the frantic babble of voices coming from the partygoers. The scent of the briney sea flowed over him, borne by the cool breeze that came off of the water. Gabriel closed his eyes as he set his feet on the asphalt and shut the van door behind him with a solid thunk.

The rush and shush of the water and the sound of his own pounding heart seemed to merge for a moment. The sensation he had felt the day of the accident, like there was a string attaching him to something out in the depths, suddenly returned. There was someplace he was supposed to go. Something amazing would be there. Gabriel's eyelids flew open. Sticky sweat coated his face. He viciously pushed the feeling away.

The storm would have found us wherever we headed. But if we had done what Mom had wanted, stayed closer to shore, they would have survived. But I insisted. And they ignored their instincts, took us out into deeper water, to please me. My fault. All my fault.

Corey was beside him. "You okay, Gabe?"

Gabriel gave him a shaky smile. "Yeah, yeah, I'm good. Just lead the way. This is your friend Jenny's party after all."

Corey grinned and rocked back and forth on his sandaled heels. "She's a real sweetheart."

"They always are, Corey. Your friends—excluding me—are like you. Bright. Sunny. Cheerful and generous."

Corey clapped him on the back. "So are *you*. Come on, let's go in. I'm dying for a beer. And just remember that you don't have to go onto the beach if you don't want to. We can stay inside the very land-bound house."

Gabriel nodded. He knew that he didn't have to go out on the beach. The thing Corey didn't understand was that he *wanted* to.

He loved the ocean. Loved it still, despite what it had taken from him. He just couldn't stand the thought of actually going in it or looking at it or even hearing it.

They walked up the front path to a brightly lit porch. People were sprawled on the porch swing with beers in their hands. Though it was still cool, most of the women wore cut off shorts and tanks. The guys were in board shorts and graphic T-shirts. There was that familiar air of wildness tinged with relief that always came when finals were over for the year. A blonde with a striped red shirt pushed a cup of warm beer into Gabriel's right hand as soon as they stepped up onto the porch. Immediately, half a dozen people crowded around Corey. Gabriel stood back and watched. Wherever he went Corey was mobbed, and Gabriel just tried not to get in the way.

Finally, a young woman with frizzy black hair, plump hips and a wasp-like waist emerged from the house. Her face lit up as soon as she caught sight of Corey. She rushed to him. "Corey!"

"Jenny!" Corey enveloped her in a hug. She gave as good as she got. "Gabe, get over here. I want to introduce you to Jenny."

Gabriel came nearer, extending his hand to Jenny, but she engulfed him in a bear hug just the same as she had given Corey.

"You're just like how Corey described you. But different than how I imagined you'd be even after reading *Swimmers in the Deep*," she said after she pulled back to study his face.

"I'm afraid of what you imagined." Gabriel gave his best friend a pointed look that said he was going to make Corey pay for this later.

She cocked her head to the side, studying him through her chunky black-rimmed glasses with a critical eye. "Actually, you're more handsome than I thought, and I was expecting really handsome."

Gabriel flushed and scrubbed at the back of his head. "Oh, thank you."

"And you're just as shy and introverted as Corey warned me

about, too." She grasped Gabriel's hands and started pulling him into the house. "But he also said that you warm up once you get to know people. So we're going to have you get to know some people."

Gabriel cast a horrified look at Corey, who was standing there with his hands laced over his large belly, smiling Buddha-like.

"What people?" Gabriel asked.

"People who are dying to meet you! They read *Swimmers* as well." She dragged him into a side room where three people were already seated, laughing and talking. Jenny pushed him into a deep recliner chair where everyone could see him. "Hey everybody, this is Gabriel Braven. Gabriel, this is everyone."

All eyes turned towards him, and he knew he was flushing more hotly than before. He wanted to hide in the leathery folds of the recliner, but there was nowhere to go. Corey sauntered into the room and splayed himself out on a loveseat.

A woman with mousy brown hair and glasses that kept sliding down to the tip of her nose asked, "So where did you get the idea for *Swimmers*?"

"That's Karen, by the way," Jenny said.

"Yeah, sorry about that! Should have introduced myself. But I've been dying to ask you about the story since I read it. We all have!" Karen said brightly.

There were a series of nods around the room. Gabriel desperately wanted to turtle in on himself, but he was trapped. "Uh, okay. Well, I got the idea for the Mers from a story my mother told me. It's sort of an urban legend where my grandmother lives."

"So they have a local merman story in that town? I'm Joe, by the way." Joe was a young man with bushy black eyebrows. He wore a pair of worn brown corduroys yet managed to make them look stylish.

"Yeah, that's where she heard it," Gabriel said.

"That's really cool. And my name's Sarah. Oh, and I've been dying to know if the love story is based on anything?" Sarah asked. She had ginger-colored hair and giggled as she looked at Gabriel shyly.

Another flare of color heated Gabriel's cheeks. "No, no, just my imagination."

"The ending was so nihilistic though," Joe said with a frown. "I mean he goes and kills himself over what could have been an optical illusion!"

"Only if you read it that way!" Karen objected, while Sarah bobbed her head in agreement. "You could also read it as *real*. That the merman was real, and that he would come and save the main character."

"There's no way to read the story as *real*," Joe scoffed. "It was like a whole metaphor for love: it's illusory and will kill you in the end."

"We have the author right here. So why don't we ask him?" Karen was the one who spoke, but all four sets of eyes turned to Gabriel.

"Authors don't get to say what the story is about. They might intend something, but the subconscious offers a lot more for the reader to see and interpret," Joe said, though he, too, was looking at Gabriel with surprising intensity.

"Well, I …" Gabriel swallowed. Words seemed beyond him at that moment. The girls were more accurate than Joe was on the surface, but after what he had said to Corey in the car, maybe Joe was correct about the ultimate meaning of the story. He didn't know what to say.

Corey saved him from answering by saying, "Some of it's real, Joe. Gabe, tell them the latest news about the dig and the Mers."

Gabriel gave his best friend a grateful look. "Uh, yeah. This past fall, my grandmother moved back to Ocean Side, the town where the legend comes from."

"She's already a councilwoman there! Grandma G gets stuff done," Corey said proudly.

"Yeah, she was part of approving and inspecting a local development on this plot of land right by the beach called the Morse Place," Gabriel explained.

Even now he could clearly recall his grandmother's excited voice over the phone as she had told him about the discovery of an ancient Native American city. The city was like nothing ever found in North America before.

"Gabriel, it's the most amazing thing," Grace had begun. "I was reluctant to grant the zoning change for the Morse Place to be developed into multi-family homes and condos. There's always been something *special* about it, not the least of it being that we found you there after—after the accident, but—but I knew it would be good for the town. So I agreed to the development. I went to see how the construction was going. They were just beginning to dig the basements and level the earth, I think. And I just … *felt* it."

Gabriel's chest had clenched when she mentioned the Morse Place. That was where he had washed up. He could remember all too clearly the expanse of beach where he had, at first thought, he had been *placed*. But monsters didn't exist. They certainly didn't carry you in their tentacles through the deep. That had been some terrible dream or hallucination he had had after the trauma of losing his parents and nearly drowning.

"What did you feel, Grandma?" he had asked her, pushing his own feelings of unease to the side.

"A sense of anticipation. As if I *knew* they would discover something and I was *waiting* for them to do it," she had answered, and his sense of unease had grown. He knew all about having feelings like hers. It never led to anything good. "I watched as they started to dig up the earth and then … it was so odd, but before I actually even saw the top of the building, I screamed for them to stop. I practically jumped in front of the machinery!"

What they had discovered was the top of a massive stone temple, buried seemingly purposefully beneath the dirt and sand. And that wasn't all they had found. There was a whole city of buildings that would have looked more at home in ancient Egypt or the Yucatan Peninsula. But beyond the shock of finding such extraordinary architecture where it had never even been suspected to exist, was discovering the unmistakable carvings that depicted two different peoples meeting. One group coming from the land and one from the sea. The people from the sea were humanoid, but the carvings showed that they lived underneath the waves. Mers.

"Obviously, they weren't really mermen and mermaids. More like a seafaring tribe, though it definitely explains where some of the old legends came from," Gabriel finished telling them an abridged version of what his grandmother had told him.

"But the kinds of structures you're talking about aren't found in North America," Karen said.

"You're correct about that. I guess it's rewriting the history books. Professor Johnson Tims of Miskatonic University is heading up the dig," Gabriel said.

"Miskatonic? Then it must be the dig my friend Greta is on!" Sarah exclaimed. "She's been so closed-mouthed about it that I didn't realize it was the same one you were describing."

"When are the people from Miskatonic anything but closed-mouthed?" Jenny asked with a roll of her eyes.

"I'm surprised Greta's still friends with you, Sarah," Karen said. "From what I hear, once a person goes to Miskatonic, they don't have time for anything but their studies and the other students there."

"And what's the deal with that?" Joe jumped in. "They act as if what they're doing is earth-shattering, yet no one there publishes. There are never any big stories out of the university. They're all poseurs, I think."

"You sound jealous," Jenny said with a wry smile.

"Every student who goes there gets a full ride. The place is bursting with money. And after they finish school, the students either continue on at the university or are placed in high-paying jobs. *Every single student*." Joe shook his head. "Their endowment is more than Harvard and Princeton's combined. It's *not* fair."

"Considering I can already feel the weight of my student loans like a physical bag of bricks on my back, I think I'm jealous, too," Jenny remarked.

Everyone nodded glumly.

"We're going to be in Ocean Side, Sarah, so maybe we'll run into Greta," Corey said.

"I'll let her know you'll be there. We do text and stuff," Sarah said with a warm smile.

The conversation then veered off onto other topics, including the professors they loved or hated and what everyone was doing over the summer. Gabriel found himself only half listening. The shush and crash of the waves was calling to him. He found himself standing before he realized he was moving at all.

"I'm just going to stretch my legs. Be back in a bit," he explained when Corey looked at him curiously.

He had to go out onto the beach. He couldn't stand being away from it any longer. *Besides, this is supposed to be good practice for when we're at the cottage tomorrow with water on three sides of us.*

Gabriel threaded his way through the countless people in the house, narrowly avoiding getting beer spilled on him three times. He let out a huge sigh of relief as he finally escaped the crowd and ducked out onto the back deck. From the deck it was only a few steps down to the beach. The tugging feeling in his chest increased. It pulled him down the steps until he suddenly realized, with a jolt, that he had one foot on the sand. He let out a shuddering breath.

I can do this. No big deal. I can do it.

Gabriel kicked off his shoes and squished his bare toes into the cool, slightly damp sand. He let out another breath that ended in a soft laugh. He was okay. So far, anyways. He lifted his head. The water was about fifty feet away.

I should go closer. I CAN get closer.

He walked past the big bonfire and kept walking until the

light from the house receded. The moon was only a sliver above him, but the stars looked like millions of pinpricks in a black sheet of paper. He stopped walking when he was a few feet from the foaming surf. He trembled with fear, or maybe it was excitement, as he stared at the black water.

It feels like home. He wasn't sure what he meant by that, except that when he looked out at the moon-tinged waves his parents' faces flashed before his mind's eye. Their bodies had never been found. In a way, the entire ocean was their grave and the sky their headstone. *I miss you guys. So much.*

He took in deep draughts of the salt-scented air. His breathing eased and he felt like he was finally able to take in a full lungful of air for the first time in months. His run times had been getting worse no matter how much or little he trained. His normally golden tan had seemed to be fading away, and even his hair had lost some of its luster.

Maybe all I needed was a good dose of sea air, Gabriel chuckled to himself.

His heart rate had slowed down to a normal rate so he decided to walk along the beach for a time rather than rush back inside. He was careful not to let his feet touch the water, though. He was feeling better about things, but he wasn't that brave.

Though I can almost imagine what it would be like to have the water rushing over my bare skin.

He had gone about one hundred yards down the beach when he spotted a pile of clothing lying on the sand. He couldn't help his grin as he realized that someone from the party had decided to go skinny dipping, or at least had stripped down to their underwear. More than one person, as he realized that there was another pile beside the first. He decided that he had best head back to the house so he didn't disturb whoever it was.

Besides, I did well. Here I am a few feet from the water and I'm perfectly calm. No panic attacks. No heart palpitations. No shortness of breath. This is good. Excellent, really.

34

That was when he heard a strangled cry for help from the water. His head jerked towards the sound. He squinted out into the darkness and strained his ears.

"Hello? Is someone out there? Do you need help?" Gabriel called.

"Help! Help!" a faint female voice called back.

"Where are you?" Gabriel's spine stiffened as if cold water had been thrown on him.

"In the water! He's—he's unconscious! I—I can't—can't get him in!" the woman cried.

Someone was drowning! "Hold on! I'll get you some help!"

He spun around to race back towards the party and get some assistance. He couldn't go in the water. He simply couldn't!

"No! Don't go! He's slipping under! I can't hold him up anymore! Please!" The voice was laced with terror.

Cold, slick sweat covered Gabriel's body. His legs felt as weak as cooked noodles. He wanted to sink down in the sand and hold his head and moan. "I can't ..."

"Please! He's slipping! He's going to die!"

Gabriel looked back towards the party. There was no one near enough to call to. He was the only one. His actions would determine this unknown man's fate.

"Honey, hang on! Please hang on!" the voice pleaded.

You are the best swimmer in your class, Gabriel. His mother's phantom voice swam up in his memory.

It's been over ten years since I touched the water. What if I freeze up out there?

You're my water baby, his mother's voice whispered. *You would live in the ocean if you could.*

"Help us! Please!" the woman cried once more.

I'm the only chance he's got. Move. Dammit. MOVE!

Sick to his stomach, with his mind in a dangerous spiral of panic and an overwhelming feeling of numbness coursing through his limbs, Gabriel somehow forced himself to move towards the voice. He forced himself to plunge into the water. The liquid hit his feet, then thighs, and then there was this *thrum*. It was as if a drum had been hit hard and the sound had rippled out into the ocean in waves. Gabriel stumbled and nearly fell to his knees.

What the hell was that?

But he didn't have a chance to think about it further, because the woman's voice rose again, "Help! Oh, God, his head's going under!"

The voice's pitiful plea had his legs working again. His skin felt like it was drinking in the water. His movements became more sure and graceful. He put his arms over his head and dove beneath the waves.

Don't think. Just do. Your body will remember, his mother's voice assured him.

As sea water closed over his head for the first time in over a decade, he was surprised how easily swimming came back to him. The slick feeling of water all around him was familiar and wondrous. He propelled himself beneath the waves, only surfacing when the water was neck-deep. A sliver of panic worked its way down his spine as the waves lapped up against his chin. But he shoved the panic down.

"Where are you?" he called. All he could see was black water and the spray of stars above him.

Mom, where's Dad?

"We're here!" Her voice was closer than before, but still far away. He could hear the exhaustion in it. She was losing her ability to stay afloat with her companion.

Don't let go of the boat, Gabriel. No matter what. Don't let go.

He looked for the bob of heads above the waterline. He saw them about another thirty feet out. He didn't think. He didn't allow himself to feel. He just swam.

I'm going to get your father. And then we'll swim back to you. We'll come back to you.

"I'm coming! Hold on!" he cried as he stroked towards them. His body moved effortlessly, cutting through the waves as if he had been swimming for all of his life and hadn't taken over ten years off. The only discomfort he experienced was in his sides. They ached, but he was too filled with adrenaline to care.

"Hurry." Her voice barely rose above the slapping of the waves.

He felt the depth of the water change, opening up below him. He was a few feet from the girl and knew that the ocean floor was ten feet beneath them.

"I'm here," he said.

Her hair was plastered to her forehead. Her breath was coming in harsh gasps. She had both arms hooked beneath the armpits of her companion. His lolling head rested against her chest.

"We were horsing around and—and somehow we got taken out so far and then ... then he went under! I think he might have inhaled some water by mistake. I don't know! I got to him, but—but he was under for *a while*." She took in a gulping breath of air that sounded like a sob.

Was Dad already dead before Mom swam out to him?

"There's a lot of undertow here. You don't need to explain. It's okay. We've just got to get you guys on land." Gabriel slung one of the guy's arms over his shoulders while the girl mirrored his actions with the other arm. "Now slow and steady. We're going to swim back towards the beach. We can do this."

She nodded, unable to speak any more. They made slow though hardly steady progress. The waves weren't large, but the undertow nipped at Gabriel's feet. He realized that they were moving more sideways than forward.

"This is what happened before!" the girl cried.

"It's okay. We're going to go with the current. We've got to swim diagonally towards shore," he instructed. Luckily, that would take them nearer to the house with the party.

She just nodded.

He tried to take more of the guy's weight. He used his powerful runner's legs to kick the water and propel them forward. While it had taken him less than five minutes to reach them, it took them nearly twenty to get back to shore. But eventually, Gabriel's feet were able to touch bottom. He had the girl swim ahead to the beach while he carried the other man in.

The people on the deck were the first to see the three emerge from the water. When the girl collapsed on the sand and cried out hoarsely for an ambulance, dozens of phones were pulled out and calls made. Gabriel tried to carry the young man towards the house, but he was dead weight. Gabriel set him down on the sand. The young man vomited up water. The girl was instantly at his side.

"Oh, God, Jim, are you all right?"

Jim gave her a watery assent. Gabriel crouched down on his other side and patted his back. The guy looked like he was going to survive. Gabriel suddenly noticed Corey bursting out of the house and onto the porch.

"Gabe! Holy shit! What happened?" Corey cried as he raced over to them from the house.

"He saved our lives," the girl said. She was only wearing her underwear, but she caught hold of Gabriel's hand and squeezed it. "Thank you."

"It's … it's okay," Gabriel said faintly.

Jenny appeared behind Corey. Her face was even paler than before. "The ambulance is on its way."

Corey thumped Gabriel's back. "Crap, Gabriel, you go out for a walk and look what happens!"

"You can't take me anywhere," Gabriel managed to get out.

He sagged back onto his haunches. Exhaustion crashed down on him. His breathing was more ragged than it had been in the water. His limbs felt terribly heavy and ungainly. The partygoers surrounded him in droves, congratulating him, thumping his shoulders. He could only nod in response. He felt so breathless and ill.

"Gabe, you're looking like you could use an ambulance too," Corey said when he pulled back to look at Gabriel critically.

"I—I think I just want to take off for home once the ambulance gets here. If that's okay," he said.

"Of course, man. No problem," Corey assured him.

Gabriel turned his head towards the water. Beyond the ill feeling, there was another feeling. A familiar feeling. Something was coming. Something amazing.

Chapter 3

SOMEONE AMAZING

Corey half-carried Gabriel back to the van after the red and blue lights of the ambulance had faded into the distance.

"Did you hear the paramedic say that Jim was going to be okay?" Corey asked.

Gabriel nodded. He was too out of breath to speak at the moment.

"Did you also hear him say that you saved both their lives?" Corey asked.

Gabriel gave him a weak smile. He forced out, "I'm glad—glad I could help."

He saw Corey wince at how winded he sounded. Gabriel gritted his teeth. He should have just nodded again. He didn't even have the strength left to hide the fact that he really wasn't well. Rescuing the couple had exhausted him, though he didn't think his tiredness could all be blamed on his harrowing swim. In fact, he had felt full of strength when he was swimming, light and able to soar through the water, but now that he was back on land he felt so incredibly heavy. Each step, weighed down by gravity, was more tiring and harder than the last. He almost longed for the return of weightlessness he had felt in the ocean.

The water still terrified him, especially when he thought of its raw power and utter ruthlessness. It would have snatched that couples' lives away tonight if he hadn't come to help them. He knew he was anthropomorphizing the water, but to him the sea was *alive*. It could be generous and kind one moment and brutal and cruel the next. And yet, he couldn't stop thinking about the freedom he had felt while swimming or his secret, almost shameful wish that there was another excuse for him to throw his fears away and throw his body into the water once more.

Then there was that weird thrum or pulse or whatever it was when I stepped into the water. Maybe that's a whole new reason to stay away from the sea.

Gabriel could still feel the ghost of that thrum. It seemed to be running through his body like the lingering vibrations that continue on long after a bell has been rung. Was the thrum just his imagination? Had he only fantasized that the thrum had raced out from him into the ocean's depths?

And is it totally crazy that I feel like something knows I got into the open water for the first time since Mom and Dad's deaths? That something is going to happen because of it? Something amazing? No, no amazing. Probably something that's more likely terrifying ...

Corey popped open the van's passenger door and Gabriel used all of his strength to lift himself up into the vehicle. After he had collapsed into the seat, Corey had to clip his seat belt closed for him. Gabriel let his eyelids slide shut then. He heard Corey get in the driver side and the rumble of the van coming to life. They drove for a while in silence. Gabriel almost fell asleep, but he could feel Corey's fear for him and it kept him conscious.

"Are you okay, Gabe?" Corey's voice was small, which was totally unnatural as there was nothing small about his best friend. "I mean, I know you're *not* okay, but … but are you *okay*? Are you going to be okay?"

"Yeah, I'm just crashing. The adrenaline is wearing off. Swimming the three of us back with that undertow took more energy than running a marathon," Gabriel explained. It was half the truth, anyways.

"Oh, *adrenaline*, and then the crash, right, of course! You *would* be exhausted." Corey sounded utterly relieved. "Why didn't I think of that?"

"Because you have your worry eyes in and are afraid I'm dying in this seat?" Gabriel snorted softly.

"I think I should try and patent the Corey Worry-Eyes," Corey joked.

"They'll look for trouble so you don't have to," Gabriel intoned before coughing. The air was so dry. He tried swallowing repeatedly to get saliva into his mouth. "We'll make a mint."

"Nice." Corey grinned. "We'll be independently wealthy and can live a life of indolence."

"We pretty much do that now," Gabriel pointed out.

"Good point. But seriously, Gabe, don't you worry. We'll crash the second we get back to the dorms, and tomorrow you'll be right as rain," Corey assured him.

"Sounds like a plan. I think I'll sleep like the dead," Gabriel said, then added with a smile, "Metaphorically speaking, of course."

"Of course." Corey laughed, too, and he was happy again.

Gabriel was relieved, because he didn't want Corey worried about him—or, more accurately, even *more* worried about him than he already was. If Corey suddenly became sure that something was really wrong with him, then Gabriel's own denial on the subject might start to crack and he would have to do something about it. And he didn't want to do anything about it at all. He wanted to ignore everything wrong with him and somehow, magically, start feeling normal again.

Normal. I miss that so much. Just feeling normal rather than exhausted all the time. Not having to worry whether I'll have the energy to go on a run or stay awake in class. Funny how I felt the closest to normal in ages—actually better than normal—in the water. If I hadn't been in an absolute panic saving those people, I might have actually enjoyed it.

Corey got them back to the dorms quickly. The parking lot was empty, as most of the students had already cleared out for the summer or were partying it up elsewhere. They trudged inside and Corey hit the button for the elevator. There was no way that Gabriel was walking up any stairs at that moment. Gabriel relished the quiet. Maybe he really would sleep like the dead. He found himself frowning. Despite his exhaustion, he was still feeling that stirring of strange excitement in his chest that he used to get when he was a kid.

Something is going to happen. Something amazing. Oh, God, stop!

He leaned against the back of the elevator as it wheezed its way to their floor.

Please brain, just stop. I want to sleep.

But the feeling only intensified and his poor exhausted body started to shake. He knew what that meant. He would sleep, but it wouldn't be a restful sleep. He would dream.

I'm going to dream of the sea tonight.

Before his parents' deaths, he had dreamed of swimming in the sea almost every night. In his dreams the sea was a beautiful, wondrous place and his own personal playground. When he woke up from those dreams, he would feel depressed that he had left the water. But after his parents' deaths, Gabriel had stopped remembering his dreams. It was as if he had locked a part of his mind away from himself. Yet even though it hadn't happened in years, he knew he would dream that night and remember it. And it would be a sea dream again. He was sure of it.

Gabriel knew that he should have made some excuse to stay

awake and avoid the sea dream as soon as Corey opened the door to their dorm room, but one look at his bed had him mumbling a good night as he collapsed on top of his lumpy mattress. His body stopped twitching the moment he touched the sheets. He felt Corey gently pull a blanket over him. He grunted his thanks, or hoped he did.

He must have immediately fallen into a dream, as the rush and shush of the ocean suddenly filled his ears and he knew he couldn't hear the sea from his dorm room. The sound surrounded him and the *thrum* returned. Gabriel's eyelids sprang open, but he wasn't staring into his pillow. He was staring out at a midnight blue void.

The sea. I'm dreaming. I'm really dreaming of being in the water again.

He was suspended, weightless, in the depths, but it was not the terrifying, crushing depths he sometimes imagined where his parents' boat had crumpled like an empty pop can as it sank to the bottom of the ocean hundreds of feet below the surface. These waters were peaceful. Gabriel drew in a breath. He could breathe easily. He moved his arms by his sides. He could move gracefully. The leaden heaviness that plagued him on land was gone. There was none of the claustrophobia he had sometimes felt in shallow water either. Instead, there was just a vast expanse of water all around him beckoning him to swim freely. Gabriel kicked his feet and began to move in the silky, dark blue sea.

I'm not afraid. I can't drown here. It's just a dream. That's all. A dream where I can be free.

Gabriel grinned as he saw small phosphorescent creatures like fish, shrimp and krill twirling around him. They performed a beautiful light show for his singular enjoyment. His smile grew, delighted by what he saw.

I'd forgotten how good these dreams are.

He spun onto his back and saw the surface of the water fifty feet above his head, but the distance didn't cause his heart to stutter.

He didn't have to worry about air. He could breathe water. He didn't need the leaden pull of land.

Will I remember this tomorrow? Will I look at the sea and think of this or think of my parents' deaths?

For a moment he thought he saw the silhouette of his parents' boat plunging down towards the ocean floor out of the corner of his eye, but when he turned his head there was nothing there but silvery moonlit water. He was alone except for the flashing fish that swam in colorful schools in the distance. He was grateful that his mind wasn't offering him his parents swimming up from the deep to see him. He knew that he couldn't imagine them as they once were, only how they had become: destroyed by the sea.

I don't want to think of that day or my parents right now. Maybe that makes me a bad person, but I—I want to just ... swim. I want to be free for one night.

Gabriel kicked his feet and reached ahead of him with his arms. His body just cut through the water. His muscles rippled beneath his skin and it felt so good. He was strong again. Well again. This was beyond feeling normal. He felt *incredible*. Suddenly, he sensed a *tug* from below. He slowed his swimming and looked down. He stopped swimming altogether, just treading water as he stared and stared and stared.

Lights. Lights from the deep. This is what I saw when our boat went down and then ... then ... something came to save me ...

Instead of the grief and fear that usually filled him at any memory of his parents' deaths, this time he felt that familiar excitement building in him instead. Something was coming. *Someone* was coming.

Someone amazing.

The lights streaked up towards him until he was surrounded by their rainbow glow. The lights embraced him, cradled him in their warmth and brilliancy. He was blinded by their intensity and had to close his eyes for a moment, but he still saw the light through his eyelids. That was when he felt a touch on his waist.

His eyelids flew open again, but the only thing he could see was the dancing rainbow colors that surrounded him. Then there was another touch. Two touches on his waist. They were hands. Someone was framing his bare waist with their hands. Powerful hands. Masculine hands. The owner of those hands must have been floating directly in front of him, but the colors kept shifting and obscuring the man from Gabriel.

Who are you? Gabriel asked. The question was only in his head, because there was no way to talk underwater, not even in dreams.

But there was an answer. A soft answer, *Home.*

Home?

Safety. Warmth. Belonging.

Those are ideas. Concepts. Not a name. Not a place. A feeling.

Come to me. Come home.

I don't have a home! Gabriel insisted. His parents' house had long ago been sold. It held too many ghosts for him to be happy there anyways. The apartments his grandmother and he had lived in had never been home either. The cottage might be the closest thing he had to one, but even that wasn't really home. He was homeless.

You do have a home. Here. With me ...

The touches became firmer. They were possessive, though still gentle. Gabriel could break free of the man's grip if he wished. He felt the man's thumbs begin to rub slow circles over his hipbones. Heat bloomed in his stomach. He had never had a dream like this, and it was thrilling and frightening at the same time.

But I want this. I want this to happen. Whatever this will be, Gabriel thought.

He boldly reached forward and his fingers encountered a powerful male chest. The hands on his waist tightened pleasurably for a moment, indicating that his touch was appreciated and welcome. Gabriel allowed his fingers to drift down the man's chest, relishing the feel of hard pecs and rippling abs under his fingertips.

It had been so long since he had been with anyone. The irony that he would dream of having sex in the water was not lost on him, but it was exactly what he needed.

Gabriel's palms glided back up the man's chest, finding the stiff nubs of his nipples. He ran his thumbs around the softer skin of the areolas before tweaking the hard nubs. The man surged against him. Gabriel felt the silken brush of the man's bare legs against his own. Another welling of heat began in his belly and spread outward in shimmering waves. Gabriel trembled and drew nearer. The man's erect cock pushed against Gabriel's belly. He nearly doubled over with desire in response as his own cock sprang to full arousal. It had been too long.

The man stroked his back, easing him past the initial roller coaster of feelings. Gabriel desperately clung to the man's powerful shoulders, but slowly his body unfurled again, relaxing, relishing the caresses. His cock was a hot bar between them. He needed to be touched. He needed to be loved. And yes, he knew what Corey would say about that last part.

The man's hands slid down to his lower back and then dropped down until they were cupping Gabriel's ass. He squeezed Gabriel's butt cheeks, letting his fingers teasingly linger between them, just above his opening. Gabriel groaned and pushed forward against that magnificent body, finally feeling everything he had only been able to map out with his hands before.

Both their cocks were sandwiched between their bellies. The man kept cupping and squeezing Gabriel's ass with one hand while his other hand moved possessively to the back of Gabriel's neck. He drew Gabriel fully against him so that there was no space left between them. The two of them were made one as they spun in the water, and the brilliant rainbow colors of the lights from the deep surrounded them as if in celebration. Strain as he might, Gabriel could not see the man's face, only the shifting hues of light.

Plush, sculpted lips were suddenly on his. The man tilted Gabriel's head expertly to the side, and then his tongue was pressing between Gabriel's lips. Gabriel eagerly opened his mouth without thought, letting his invisible lover's tongue inside. The man tasted of the sea, salt and sunshine. The lazy tangle of their tongues together brought up a nearly forgotten wish for things that had never happened, for a boyfriend who would kiss him with the rush of waves in his ears and heated sand beneath his bare back. These were the summer kisses that he had always longed for but never had because he had never allowed anyone to get so close.

Gabriel grabbed the man, clutching him as if he were worried the man was going to escape. Gabriel opened his mouth wider, wanting the man's tongue deeper inside of him, as if he could devour this experience with a kiss. The man did not struggle against him, but instead met him passion for passion. They spun once more in the water, and Gabriel felt like laughing that their ardor had them twirling weightlessly in the sea.

The kiss ended and the man rested his forehead against Gabriel's. There were no puffs of breath against his face, not even bubbles to tickle his nose, but Gabriel could feel the man's certain presence, his complete oneness with this moment and with Gabriel.

The man drew back and Gabriel's mouth opened as if to call out to him. But then the man leaned back in to tenderly kiss both of Gabriel's temples. Gabriel ran his hands down the man's muscular arms, relishing the interplay of muscle covered by velvety skin. The man placed more kisses all over Gabriel's face, ending in a soft suck on the right side of his jaw. Gabriel tilted his head back so that the man could kiss and lick and suck as much as he wanted. The man obliged. He placed a chain of kisses down Gabriel's neck and lingered at the hollow at the base of Gabriel's throat.

The man's powerful hands then fastened around the backs of Gabriel's thighs. He effortlessly drew Gabriel's legs up and apart, positioning them so that they were wrapped around his waist. Heat once again coursed through Gabriel like molten lava as he felt the slightest press of the man's penis against his ass. A tentative stillness fell between them then. The man wanted permission to do more. Gabriel answered him with action. He wound his arms around the man's neck and kissed him hard and desperately while he pushed down against that teasing cock. He wanted this. He wanted a connection with someone, and if he could only have it here, in his dreams, then so be it.

One of the man's hands reached around until his fingers skimmed over Gabriel's opening. His pointer finger traced the tight swirl of muscle. Gabriel moaned almost pitifully. His cock pulsed with pleasure. As the man pushed his finger inside, Gabriel thrust down to meet it. He felt the ecstasy of being breached for the first time in years.

Even in his dreams, his sphincter was incredibly tight. The man pulled his finger out and wiggled it back in. Unlike in real life, the finger moved smoothly without the mess of using a lubricant. It was almost like his body had prepared itself naturally for the penetration.

Gabriel leaned back, his hands laced around the man's muscular neck. The water let him hold the position without strain. He squeezed his thighs around the man's waist. A second finger joined the first inside of him. Those fingers pumped in and out of him in a heady rhythm. Gabriel loved the feeling of being filled, of having his tender tissues spread. The fingers scissored, stretching him, pleasuring him. But it wasn't enough. He needed the man's cock.

As if in answer to his prayers, the man positioned the tip of his cock against Gabriel's opening. Gabriel drew in a breath and held it. The man tapped his cock against Gabriel's opening, but did nothing more until Gabriel let that breath go and allowed his body to relax. Bubbles streaked through the lights above his head.

He doesn't want to hurt me.

Gabriel didn't know if he wanted to laugh or cry at that moment. Instead of doing either, he kissed the man once more. The man kissed him eagerly back. He then pressed the head of his cock against Gabriel's opening and, with one slow steady thrust, pushed inside. There was that pleasure-pain, that feeling of being totally filled, that sex always brought, but this time there was no sense of emptiness in him as it happened. This man was not just using his body for pleasure. There was a connection between them that made it so Gabriel could never feel or be empty so long as the man was touching him. Gabriel's fingers flexed against the back of the man's neck. Neither of them moved until Gabriel relaxed against him.

Move. Please, move. I need to feel you claiming me.

The man held Gabriel to him tenderly before shifting his grip to Gabriel's waist. He drew his cock out of Gabriel's body an inch at a time. Gabriel wanted to bear down even though he knew that would stop the glorious slide of the man's cock in and out of him. He tried to just abandon himself to the sensations, to let his body be taken without fighting or controlling it, but it was so hard to just let go.

The man's cock was almost all the way out of him, only the head remaining inside. Gabriel dug his fingers into the man's shoulders. He didn't want to be abandoned. Not now. But then the man was sliding inside him again. He went so deep that Gabriel would have sworn the man's cock touched the very core of him. Gabriel's mouth opened at the force of the thrust and a watery gasp exited his parted lips.

With you. I'm with you, the man's sultry voice rang through his mind.

The man picked up the rhythm of his thrusts. Every inward thrust had his balls slapping against Gabriel's ass. Every outward pull had Gabriel keening and gripping the man harder around the waist with his thighs. The man's thrusts changed from long and silky to short and choppy. He angled his hips so that his cock rubbed against different parts of Gabriel's back passage. When the head of the man's cock dragged over his prostate, Gabriel's own cock surged between them. He felt the heat of his precum warm the water around the tip of his cock as it leaked out.

The man suddenly grasped Gabriel's cock and started to

stroke it. Gabriel curled against him once more as having his cock touched while he was being claimed became too much for him to bear. The heat between his legs built into a roaring fire. He raked his fingers down the man's back as his balls drew up tight against his body.

The man's thrusts were almost brutal now, but they were what Gabriel needed. Each inward push had the head of the man's cock rubbing Gabriel's prostate, nearly making him weep with pleasure. The hand on his cock stroked faster and faster, the thumb rubbing over the tip, spreading the slit as more precum gushed out.

Gabriel kissed the man's cheeks, chin and nose before locating his lips. They opened, allowing him entrance. Gabriel's tongue slipped inside. Salt, sweetness, sunshine. They kissed and kissed and kissed as Gabriel bore down on the man's cock, keeping it inside of him as deep as it would go. He felt the man's penis pulse and knew that he was about to cum even as Gabriel found his own orgasm spilling over him like a tidal wave. If the lights from the deep hadn't continued to blind him, he knew he would have seen his semen clouding the midnight blue water between them. There was a pulse of liquid heat inside of his body, and his own cock jerked once more and released another stream of semen in response. The man continued to stroke him, to milk him, to ease that last bit of cum out of him with his strong hand while he came in Gabriel. And their kiss continued unbroken throughout it all. Gabriel would not have broken that kiss for the world.

The man's hand only left Gabriel's cock after the last drop of semen had been wrung from him. He immediately moved that hand to Gabriel's back and slowly started caressing him up and down in long slow strokes, his tenderness as much a turn on as his forcefulness earlier had been. Gabriel's body was still shaking with aftershocks, but the soothing touches eased him and he slumped against the man's larger body, totally spent.

However, Gabriel was still clenching down on the man's cock, not wanting it to leave his body and end their physical connection. The man kissed him slowly, almost dreamily. Gabriel pressed his face against the man's throat and wrapped his arms around that powerful frame. They slowly spun in the calm sea, floating without the painful pull of gravity. Gabriel could feel that he was going to slip out of the dream soon and into the darkness of full sleep. He wanted to hang on, but the man kissed his temple as if to tell him it was okay to let go, to rest.

Words that were not Gabriel's own echoed through his mind once more. *I will not leave you. I will never leave you.*

That's because you aren't real. You can't leave me if you were never here in the first place, Gabriel replied with a sad smile.

I am real. And I will never leave you.

Despite Gabriel's rational mind telling him that this was only a dream, a part of him clung to those words. He did not want to lose this connection, this feeling. He held the thought to him tightly as he slipped from the silvery waters into blackness.

For one moment, when he woke up in the morning, Gabriel thought he felt the man's phantom embrace. Even with sunlight streaming down on him and his eyes open, clearly showing him that the dorm bed was empty except for him, Gabriel still felt he was not alone.

I will not leave you. I will never leave you.

Gabriel sighed. *If only that were true.*

Chapter 4

OCEAN SIDE

 'm fine, Corey."

"How can you see me looking at you when your eyes are closed, Gabe?"

Gabriel slowly let his eyelids open. The sun was sinking behind the hills so it wasn't terribly bright anymore. He gave his best friend a soft smile. "You have your worry eyes in again."

Corey tapped the steering wheel of the van as they cruised along the highway. "I can't help it! You look so …"

"So what?" Gabriel still felt tired, but his mind kept going

54

back to the dream he had had the night before, and each time some of his exhaustion would drain away.

Even though it was just a dream. And a dream is a dream is a dream. Important part is that it is not real.

"Fragile," Corey confessed. "You look fragile."

Gabriel gently knocked his best friend's arm. "Fragile? I am so not fragile. I'm going to have to kick your ass at something just for that comment."

"Beach run? Volleyball tournament?" Corey asked.

Both of those things had Gabriel feeling breathless just thinking of doing them. "After a few days of my grandmother's cooking and sleeping for more than four hours a night, I'll be as good as new. You'll see, and then I'll beat you at those things and more."

"I'll hold you to that, Gabe," Corey said as he adjusted the volume on the radio.

Gabriel blinked sleepily and stretched his arms over his head, dislodging the sweatshirt that Corey had tucked around him. He had been drifting in and out of sleep the entire car ride to his grandmother's. He hadn't had any more dreams like the one last night. He blushed as he realized that half the reason sleep was so appealing to him was because there was a chance he might slip back into that dream and see the man again, *really* see him. Glimpsing that face would be better than kissing or making love.

What am I thinking? That if I see his face I'll be able to find him in real life? So not going to happen. It was just a dream.

He knew that nothing in reality could match that dream. Gabriel shook his head to clear it. He looked out the window and realized that they were on the Sea Spray Highway, which had gotten its name because it ran along the coast. Gabriel's gaze drifted towards the ocean, which was about one hundred feet away. The waves were rolling in. They were three feet tall. The surf was choppy, with a ton of white caps. As a kid, he would have longed to dive right in and ride those waves. His parents would have worried about the undertow, but Gabriel had never been afraid of the water. He always seemed to instinctively know the currents. Maybe that had helped him survive when his parents had drowned.

"We're almost there," Gabriel murmured, recognizing a bright McDonald's sign. The sign was about ten miles from Ocean Side. "I didn't realize I'd slept so long."

"Yeah, you were really out of it." Again, there was a worried little frown on Corey's pudgy face.

"Last night just took it out of me. Adrenaline, remember?" Gabriel murmured.

"Yeah. Grandma G is going to *freak* when she hears what you did. A hero! A watery rescue! You were something else," Corey enthused once more.

Gabriel picked up his 2-litre bottle of water from the van's cup holder. It was already half gone. He chugged the remainder. His mouth still felt dry and cottony. "I can't really believe it myself."

"I just want to say how absolutely amazing you were last night," Corey raved. "I mean, going in after those people when you've been terrified of water forever. You saved their lives! You are awesome, my man!"

Gabriel gave him a wan smile. "So you've said about a million times already, but thank you, though it was more instinct than conscious heroism."

"It deserves to be said a million more times," Corey responded, undaunted.

"I'm just glad they were all right," Gabriel murmured.

Corey moved the van over into the right hand lane, preparing to get off at their exit. "Do you think your water phobia is conquered?"

Gabriel turned his head towards the water. His chest clenched and his stomach tightened just looking at it, but there was a tingle of excitement that ran through him as well.

What am I thinking? That I'll meet a mystery lover in the

56

water? So crazy.

He firmly looked away from the sea. Besides the fact that such a thought was crazy, finding any pleasure in the ocean felt like a betrayal of his parents.

They wouldn't have been out there that day but for me. They wouldn't have gone to that spot. They wouldn't have died.

"Gabe? You still with me?" Corey glanced over at him.

"Yeah, yeah, still a little zoned. I don't think I'll be going swimming for fun just yet," he said, yet even as his lips formed the word "swimming" his heart gave a fluttering leap as he imagined running into the water and diving into the waves and then … then someone's arms embracing him, welcoming him home.

Someone amazing.

"Here's our exit," Corey said as he steered the van to the right and followed the sloping exit ramp towards Ocean Side.

"Turn left at the bottom of the ramp then keep going straight. The cottage is right on the ocean. You won't be able to miss it," Gabriel said.

"Affirmative." Corey was practically bouncing in his seat as he took that final turn.

Gabriel knew that Corey loved his grandmother as much as Gabriel himself did. Sometimes he thought Grace loved Corey just a little more than she loved even him, which Gabriel completely understood. Corey was family in every sense of the word.

"You know, I wanted you to come with us that summer," Gabriel said, his throat going tight as he made that confession.

Corey's bright brown gaze skittered over to him. "What?"

"The year my parents died, I wanted you to come with us. You could have been with us on the boat that day if I'd had my way. At the time, I was really bummed you weren't there. Now, of course, I'm so glad you weren't," Gabriel explained. His hands tightened into fists in his lap. He could have lost both his parents and Corey. He wouldn't have survived that.

"Gabe." Corey looked and sounded like a wounded puppy.

"It's just, you're finally here, you know? In Ocean Side. You and me. Just like I wanted back then. I hope this is a *good* time for you. I want it to be." Gabriel shifted in his seat. "I don't want this all to be about me *remembering* my parents and—and *mourning* them, you know?"

Corey squeezed his shoulder. "You can mourn them as much as you need to. If you want to talk about them, I'm ready to listen. It's healthy."

"I'm not going to spend our vacation being maudlin. It's just—look, there's the cottage!" Gabriel didn't finish his thought, instead he just pointed through the windshield to a small blue and white cottage that sat out on a jut of land. It was isolated from the rest of the town by the road and the water. It was a beautiful spot, though Gabriel's stomach seemed to drop into his feet at the sight.

Corey slowed the van down and pulled into the short gravel drive. The front door opened as soon as he turned off the engine. Gabriel's grandmother stepped out onto the front porch. She waved happily. Her white hair was cut in a sleek bob that accentuated her beautiful face.

"Gabriel! Corey! Oh, I'm so glad you're both here!" she cried out.

Both young men tumbled out of the van. Corey was closest to Grace, and he immediately swept the small woman up in a bear hug and spun her around. She squealed in pleasure like a young girl instead of the sixty-five year old librarian and town councilwoman she was.

"Corey! Put me down, you silly boy," she laughed, not sounding like she wanted him to release her at all, but Corey complied. As soon as she was let go, she raced over to Gabriel and cupped his face in her hands. "Oh, Gabriel, how I've missed you."

"I missed you too, Grandma," he responded softly.

She kissed him on the cheek gently then pulled back and gazed at him with such love that he found himself looking down uncomfortably.

"Well, let's not stand around out here. I've got dinner cooking!" she said, sparing him.

"Oooh! What did you make?" Corey asked.

"Your favorites. Beef stew, homemade mashed potatoes, sweet corn on the cob and for dessert ..."

"Cherry pie? Please tell me you made your world-famous pie!" Corey rocked forwards and backwards in excitement.

"Yes, of course. Always for you." She patted Corey's shoulder.

"If you start giggling like a little girl right now, Corey, I promise to record you and post it all over the Internet. You'll never live it down," Gabriel said.

"For your grandmother's pie, I'd post it myself," Corey said sagely.

"Well, get on in then!" She shooed the boys towards the house.

"Wait, we've got to bring our stuff in," Gabriel said. He almost laughed when he saw Corey's crestfallen face. "How about you go inside, Corey, and I'll grab a few things we'll need for tonight?"

Corey immediately brightened, but then he said, "No, Gabe, you should go in. I know you're, uh ..." He paused. He then glanced at Grace and then back at Gabe meaningfully, before adding, "I know you're not feeling too good after ... your *incredible* rescue of those people last night!"

"What? Rescue?" His grandmother looked between the two young men, wanting an explanation.

"Oh, it was *epic*, Grandma G! Gabriel saved two people's lives! He saved them from *drowning*!" Corey exclaimed, even though he looked slightly shamefaced as he then said to Gabriel, "I know you probably wanted to be the one to tell her, but I just couldn't hold it in."

"It's fine, Corey. You'll tell it better than I would anyways," Gabriel said with an understanding smile.

"Gabriel went into the *water*?" his grandmother asked. One of her hands actually crept up to her throat as if she could feel the water rising around her.

Corey nodded. "He *swam* out to them!"

"That's—that's *incredible*, Gabriel!" Grace stared at him with a mixture of shock and pride on her face.

"But it sort of took it out of him," Corey said. "He's been pretty run down since then."

"Corey!" Gabriel hissed. Why did his best friend have to say that?"

His grandmother immediately put one of her delicate hands against his forehead, feeling for a fever. He gently shook her off.

"You do look a little peaked. Do you want to go lie down?" she asked.

Gabriel shook his head and took a step back. "No, I'm good. Seriously. I just want to stretch my legs a bit before going in."

"If you're sure," she said uncertainly.

Corey, too, looked unconvinced, but Gabriel said, "Go on. I'm fine. Really. I'll be there in a minute."

Corey put an arm around Grace's shoulders and they both headed inside as he told her more about Gabriel's amazing rescue. Gabriel let out a soft sigh as soon as the door closed. His shoulders slumped and he raked a hand through his hair. He was glad to have a moment alone. It was exhausting trying to act normal in front of his grandmother. He closed his eyes, and suddenly, the sound of the waves was all he could hear. He roused himself and went quickly to the back of the van. He would get the bags and be done with it. However, he found himself casting one last look back at the ocean.

The sea was a dark blue going towards black in the light of the dying day. The whitecaps were creamy like the foam on a cappuccino. He saw a single light shining at the top of a sailboat's mast in the far distance. He started walking towards the water. He didn't notice when the gravel turned to soft sand. He only stopped when the sand became hard and packed from being soaked by the waves. He could feel the pull again, that tug at the center of his chest towards that same spot.

That boat is right over where ours went down. Our boat is still there. In the darkness. Crushed by the pressure. Are my parents' bodies down there, too? No, they would have floated. Been eaten by fish and—

"Gabriel?" His grandmother's voice broke him out of his dark thoughts. He spun around. His grandmother was standing a few feet away from him. "I didn't mean to scare you, but I was calling for some time. Dinner's on the table."

Gabriel blinked. Over her shoulder, he saw Corey getting their things out of the van. He glanced back out at the water. It was too dark to see anything anymore. He had been standing there far longer than he thought.

"Sorry, Grandma. I sort of lost track of time."

She put a comforting hand on his arm. "Corey told me more about what happened last night. You saved those people, Gabriel. You leaped into that water and saved them," she said. "What was it like getting back in the water after all these years?"

Gabriel again remembered the thrum. It and the pull seemed related somehow. For one moment, he was tempted to dip his foot into the water to see if it happened again.

If it is a signal then he'll know I'm here. Wait, he? The man in my dream or someone else?

He shook himself again. "It was … good, I guess?"

"Are you all right, Gabriel?" she asked.

He shrugged, giving her his most bland look. "I'm good. Just a little tired after finals. But like I told Corey, a few days in the sun and I'll be back to myself in no time."

"Will you?" She put a hand on his arm. "I was worried about moving back here."

"Grandma, I'm fine with it—"

"It wasn't just you I was worried about. I was worried about myself, too." She drew her thin white sweater closer around her. "I couldn't even look at the sea for years after—after it happened. I was almost grateful when the doctor advised us to move away for your sake. So you see, it wasn't only for you that we did that. I know now it was very unfair of me to act as if it was."

Gabriel was quiet for a moment before saying, "I was having screaming nightmares. I was a mess. You were holding everything together. You had already raised your son. Suddenly, you had another one to raise, but unlike Dad, I was a basket case."

She cupped his cheek. "Losing John and Kate was the worst moment of my life. But having you, in my house, with me every day, has been one of life's greatest blessings."

Gabriel swallowed hard. "I know that it was a burden to bring me up."

"Burden? No, Gabriel, it's been a joy!" she cried. "And I'm so proud of you. The only thing I wish …"

He looked up at her. She had caught her lower lip in her teeth, and her doubt about saying whatever was on her mind was as clear as day for him to read. Something clenched in his chest.

"What do you wish, Grandma?" he asked softly, even as he dug his fingernails into his palms.

"That you could meet someone special. John's life was so very happy after he met Kate. Your mother made him … *shine*," she said with a fond smile on her face.

He smiled, remembering how his parents had still been so in love after fifteen years of marriage that it was like no one else existed at times. They knew what each other was thinking without the other one ever having to say it. His father would suddenly break away from whatever he was doing to seek his mother out whenever she needed him, even though she hadn't asked for help. But it was always exactly when she had needed him. For one moment, he thought of his dream from the night before. It was ridiculous to compare a dream to his parents' everyday reality, but the caring words, the statement that the man would never leave him, was exactly like something his father and mother would say to one another. He felt his chest tighten.

"I used to be so embarrassed by them acting all lovey dovey. Why couldn't they ignore one another like other kids' parents did? I didn't get it back then how special that was. How rare," Gabriel murmured.

"I want you to have that love for yourself, Gabriel. I see how you keep yourself apart from others. It's as if you're observing life from a safe distance. I don't want that isolation for you," she said softly.

"I'm not alone, Grandma. I have you. I have Corey," Gabriel told her, trying to make her understand that it was enough. He wasn't going to find a love like his parents had had. Even if there was someone out there for him, they would have to get through his Fort Knox-like defenses, and who would want to spend their time doing that? No one in their right mind. He would just forever have his longing, his writing and, maybe, his occasional vivid dreams to release the pressure of being alone whenever it built up too much. That was enough.

"Corey is a dear. Speaking of which, he probably has gotten his fingers in the cherry pie already. We had best go in before he devours the whole thing," his grandmother said. Then she got a mischievous look on her face. "Lucky for us, I baked two and hid the other one in the refrigerator behind the milk!"

Gabriel laughed. He linked his arm with hers and they walked back to the cottage.

Chapter 5

HISTORY IS PRICELESS

*A*fter dinner, Gabriel helped Corey bring the rest of their stuff in from the van and then collapsed on his bed in his old room. Not even the sound of the waves, or Corey's snoring in the room next door, could keep him up. Unlike the night before, he had no dreams, which was only slightly depressing. He slept like the dead until after ten o'clock and awoke to blue skies and sunshine pouring through his bedroom windows. He quickly showered and dressed before taking the stairs two at a time to the ground floor. He found Corey at the kitchen table with the remnants of breakfast before him and his grandmother at the sink.

For one moment, his mind flashed back to the last time he had breakfast in this kitchen: his parents looking at each other over their coffee cups, his grandmother smiling and shaking her head at the three of them, and the eternal lure of the sea. His old seat was vacant. As he looked at it, he felt a stirring in his chest. It was the old excitement.

Something is going to happen. Something amazing. Gabriel swallowed the thick bile that suddenly rose up in his throat. *God, I hope not.*

"Gabriel! You're up!" his grandmother called brightly.

Gabriel's gaze snapped up from his old chair to her. He tried to remember the good feeling he had had before coming into the kitchen and put it in a smile for her. He only half succeeded. "Not quite as bright and early as the two of you."

Corey had evidently already polished off a plate of scrambled eggs. He was looking mournfully at his last piece of toast, clearly debating whether he wanted another piece after this one. His grandmother's dishes were already clean and drying beside the sink. The smell of eggs, bacon and butter hung pleasantly in the air. Gabriel's stomach rumbled.

His grandmother let out a laugh when she heard it. "What would you like to eat, Gabriel?"

"Oh, I can get myself something," he assured her.

"No, let me." She held up a hand when he opened his mouth to protest. "I'm not offering to feed you for totally altruistic purposes." She lit a burner under a fresh pan. "I have plenty of work for you today. If you're feeling up to it."

His grandmother and Corey's gazes met for a brief moment. They had clearly been talking about his poor health. Corey hadn't completely bought the adrenaline explanation for why he had become so sick after swimming.

Gabriel did some jumping jacks to demonstrate how well he felt. He was slightly breathless afterwards, but he quickly hid it. "I feel fantastic, actually. A good night's sleep did the trick."

She looked him over critically, but finally nodded. "All right, but I want you to stop and rest if you start to feel ill again."

"I promise."

"I need you to sort through the basement. The entire history of the Braven clan is down there," she said.

Gabriel felt a stirring of excitement at the thought of digging through the Braven family's history. His grandmother's love of the past had rubbed off on him. "I'm ready to begin."

"You might not be so eager after you are covered in the dirt and grime of several decades. That's minimally how long some of that stuff has been down there. So we need to fortify you," she said. "Eggs and toast?"

"Sounds great." Gabriel avoided his old chair and sat instead in the one his mother had always occupied. He wished he could feel her presence through it, but it was just a piece of wood and held nothing of her spirit.

"You made your husband take the Braven name, didn't you, Grandma G?" Corey asked, then gave a hoot when she put another hot piece of buttered toast on his plate.

"I did." She nodded.

"That was very modern of you," Corey said.

"The Bravens have been here for over three hundred years. I would have been the last otherwise. Besides, his surname was Smith. Nothing wrong with Smith, but it didn't quite have the same ring to it," she said.

"Grace Smith. Gabriel Smith. John Smith. Nah, definitely doesn't have the same ring as Braven," Corey agreed.

"How did you sleep, Corey?" Gabriel asked.

"Like a baby on Nyquil," he laughed. "I got up at the same time as Grandma G a couple hours ago. We've been talking about the dig. Man, I think you're going to need to write a sequel to *Swimmers*."

"What do you mean?" Gabriel asked.

"Johnson has fully unearthed the temple and I've already been inside." His grandmother set a glass of fresh-squeezed orange juice down in front of him. "It's magnificent."

"Sounds amazing. But I thought they just started the

excavation. Don't archeologists dig down like one inch at a time and then sift the dirt so they don't miss anything?" Gabriel asked as his forehead furrowed. From his grandmother's description of the temple, he imagined it must be several stories tall.

"Johnson has ruffled some feathers with his *aggressive* techniques at the site. But how long do people think the developers are going to wait before bulldozing the whole thing?" She shook her head. "The developers are already in court seeking a ruling that they be allowed to get back to work building their condos. Miskatonic has a lot of pull, but it isn't infinite. The more Johnson uncovers of the settlement, the more weight will be given to this being a unique historical site. And it is *unique*."

Gabriel took a swig of orange juice, rolling the pulp against the roof of his mouth, relishing the tartness. "Sounds like he's doing the right thing then."

His grandmother put a pat of butter in the pan to cook his eggs as she answered, "Yes, but it's been contentious, as these things always are."

"Grandma G, you're burying the lede! Tell him about the inscription inside the temple about the Mer people," Corey said with a waggle of his eyebrows.

"There's an inscription? I didn't think that any Native American tribes had written languages, except for the Cherokee," Gabriel pointed out. "Is it Cherokee? Is that how Johnson translated it so fast?"

"It isn't Cherokee," his grandmother answered as she cracked two eggs into the pan and they began to sizzle. "The group that built the settlement is a wholly unknown tribe. But my understanding is that the language used in the inscription is similar to another one that the scholars at Miskatonic were already familiar with, so the translation is going very quickly. Johnson will be able to explain this to you far better than I. Ask him to tell you about it at dinner tonight."

"He's coming here?" Gabriel's interest perked up.

"Johnson Tims is Grandma G's boyfriend," Corey informed him *sotto voce*.

"What?" Gabriel squawked. He was aware that his grandmother and the professor knew one another, but not that they were dating. His grandmother had rarely dated since a heart attack had killed his grandfather the year Gabriel was born. Though his father had urged her to find someone special, she had responded that relationships like the one she had had with her husband were a "gift, not a given" and she didn't expect lightning to strike twice. Had it now with this Johnson Tims?

"Ah! One yolk broke! Gabriel, don't shout or your breakfast will be ruined," she chided him as she moved to put some bread in the toaster. "Johnson is a *friend*. That's all. For now. I think you'll like him, though he's a little ... gruff. Comes from being in the military, I think."

"I want to meet him. I'll keep an open mind, but he has to pass inspection," Gabriel said. If this guy was dating his grandmother, he needed to check him out. "So tell me about this inscription."

"Well, they've only translated part of it and he hasn't even told me all they've discovered. But I do know that it mentions the Mers."

"Mers like your swimmers in the deep. Mermen and mermaids! Not humans!" Corey burst in.

"Oh, you! You're making it sound silly but it's really quite fascinating, and for Johnson it's deadly serious." She ground pepper and salt over the eggs.

"And Johnson is a deadly serious dude." Corey nodded sagely.

Gabriel laughed. His grandmother set a plate of eggs and toast down in front of him. He eagerly tucked in. "So what does this inscription say about the Mers?"

She began to clean the stove as she answered, "Supposedly, the Mers—and as Corey said, they were not considered human—

would come ashore to meet with the tribe."

"Tell him about the loving! Don't forget that!" Corey crowed.

Gabriel's eyebrows rose up into his hairline. "Is that in the inscription, or is this part of Corey's delusional need to put love into everything?"

"Corey is correct. The Mers and the tribe exchanged gifts, ideas and ... uhm, well, people." His grandmother blushed. "The Mers were apparently very beautiful."

Gabriel's fork paused halfway up to his mouth. Golden yolk dripped down onto the plate. "You mean they married and—"

"Had half-human, half-Mer babies! Didn't they go over this with you in health class?" Corey asked.

"Interspecies breeding? No, no, they didn't," Gabriel said. "What kind of health classes did you take?"

"The fun ones!" Corey chortled.

"The Mers were undoubtedly just a seafaring tribe and very human, just like the rest of us. But it's fascinating in its own right, even without the mermaids," she said.

"Or mermen for our Gabriel here," Corey chuckled.

"Ha ha. Are you saying my situation is so dire that I need to start looking at a different species for love?" Gabriel gave Corey a mock outraged look, but he felt a flush come to his cheeks as he thought of his dream of being with the man in the water.

"Hey, we've got to get you interested in *someone*. Maybe a merman is the trick," Corey said.

"With my fear of water, I'm sure that's just the thing for me. Talk about star-crossed love," Gabriel said.

"You never know," Corey teased. "Love is in the air!"

"You're always saying that. What is it with you and trying to set people up these days?" Gabriel asked. It wasn't like Corey needed to live vicariously through others. He was constantly dating, and had more girls after him than he knew what to do with.

Corey threaded his fingers over his stomach, looking like a

serene Buddha. "My purpose is to spread joy and well wishes wherever I go."

"Just so you know, Gabriel, the Native Americans were not the only people romanced by the Mers." His grandmother's eyes twinkled eerily like Corey's. "Supposedly, some of the people in this town have been as well. So your idea behind *Swimmers* wasn't completely unique."

"You're kidding!" Gabriel let out a laugh.

She shook her head. "Over the years there have been urban legends about beautiful people from the sea seducing many a person."

Corey perked up. "What about the Bravens? Do they have any fishy blood?"

Something in Gabriel's chest twisted. If the Bravens really did have Mer blood, would his father have drowned? It was a ridiculous idea anyways. Mers were not real.

His grandmother grew thoughtful and slightly sad. Gabriel wondered if she was thinking the same thing. "Every family has its dark secrets, Corey. But if the Mers ever touched the Bravens, it wasn't deeply enough. After all, I love the sea, but I've never been able to breathe underwater."

"Still doesn't mean that Gabriel can't find a little *Mer love*," Corey sang.

"I think I'm ready to work now, since I'm sure we won't get anything but unwanted dating advice from Corey for the rest of the morning," Gabriel said. His plate was sparkling clean. He had devoured his breakfast with an appetite that surprised even him. Maybe he *did* just need some brisk ocean air and sunshine to get back to his normal healthy self.

"Go on down and look around. I'll join you in a moment after I clean up the dishes." His grandmother opened the door to the basement and flipped on the light switch. A small pool of yellow light came on at the very base of the wooden stairs.

"What about Corey? Isn't he joining me in this task?"

Gabriel asked.

Corey stuck his tongue out at him as he helped bring the remainder of the breakfast dishes over to the counter to be cleaned.

"He's going to be sorting through some boxes of books in the attic," she said. "I figure divide and conquer. We'll get things done more quickly this way."

"Hmmm, sounds logical," Gabriel said.

"Don't worry about the dishes, Grandma G. I'll do them. You go down with Gabe," Corey offered.

"All right. Thank you, Corey," she said.

Gabriel hiked down the stairs first, only slowing as he reached the bottom. That was when he understood the magnitude of his task. There was only a single bare bulb, which hung in the center of the basement. The basement was one large room that stretched out amoeba-like beneath the entirety of the house. Hulking towers of boxes sprouted up everywhere like trees in a forest.

"Overwhelming, isn't it?" his grandmother said as she walked down the wooden stairs and stood beside him in the pool of warm yellow light.

"Uh, yeah, a little." Gabriel rubbed the back of his neck. "I can see why you wanted help with it."

She laughed lightly. "I've been putting it off way too long. But I think that the time to go through and purge what's isn't necessary is ripe. A new start."

"So while I'm pawing through this stuff, you have Corey looking at paperbacks?" Gabriel asked.

"I'm giving most of them to the library and the assisted living home. As a librarian, I feel it's my duty to make sure that books continue having a shelf life for as long as possible," she said.

"You know that Corey will totally get caught up in reading them and get nothing done?" he asked with a wry grin.

"True, but we have all summer. Getting lost in a good book is a completely acceptable pastime in my opinion." She glanced quickly at her watch. With a grimace, she added, "I hate to put an enormous task in front of you and leave, but …"

"You've got plans?" he asked, bumping her shoulder affectionately with his own. "Something for the library? Or does it have something to do with Professor Tims?"

She blushed again and playfully slapped his arm. "I am going to see Johnson at the dig site for the monthly inspection, if you must know." She patted her hair.

"Oh, ho ho! You've got a date!" Gabriel exclaimed. "All this talk about *me* needing someone special, and you neglected to mention that *you've* found someone. I really have to check out this Johnson Tims."

She colored more deeply. "Maybe experiencing my own happiness at finding a—a *friend* made me wish that you had one, too."

"Why didn't you mention this before?" he asked.

"I was going to. I guess I was afraid to jinx it. My goodness, it's been so long for me that I hardly know what I'm doing," she confessed.

"You've still got it, Grandma. I'm sure he's in your thrall," Gabriel teased her.

She shook her head, laughing girlishly, and touched her nicely styled hair again. "Don't tease me too much, Gabriel, I don't know if I can take it. Do you think you'll be okay down here?"

He ticked off on his fingers the instructions she always gave him in regards to possible history. "Throw out stuff that doesn't have anything to do with our family history. Make sure to separate out any photographs. And keep my eyes and mind open to all the rest. History is priceless."

"History is priceless," she agreed, repeating her favorite tagline.

"Words to live by. Okay, go, get out of here and enjoy your date," he said, gesturing for her to go up the stairs.

"Don't work all day, Gabriel. I also want you to have fun," she said. She patted his cheek, and with a waft of her rose perfume she was gone.

Gabriel looked around him again. There had to be over a hundred boxes, half a dozen bureaus, two or three roll-top desks, and who knew what else down here for him to go through. His grandmother wouldn't be content until every single paper had been looked at and then catalogued. He would put the things he thought should be tossed out in a pile for her to go through before they actually threw anything away. His grandmother had a better eye for what should be trashed or salvaged than he did.

"Now where the heck to start?" He let out a soft laugh and grabbed the nearest box.

A few hours later he was sitting with his back against one pile of boxes while he pawed through boxes from another. His eyes were watering and his nose was running as a century's worth of dust rose up from the bills he was paging through.

"Who the hell thinks their dairy bills from the 1940s are worth saving?"

He tossed the bills back into the box and kicked it away from him. So far he had managed to find ancient bills, tons of back issues of *National Geographic* and scribbled grocery lists. He doubted any of it was precious history. Not to mention it was boring as dirt. With a sigh, he sat there idly letting his gaze roam around him. He froze when his eyes hit upon a hand carved box that was half-hidden beneath a bureau. It looked far different than anything else he had gone through so far. He scooted along the floor until he could grab the edge of it. It felt heavy.

"Definitely not just papers in here," he murmured.

The top of the box was carved with a graceful sunfish surrounded by glued-on seashells. The arched lid reminded him of a treasure chest. There were two brass hinges that had turned green due to age. He flipped the lid back.

Inside was jewelry. The jewelry was made of delicate shells strung on thin silver wire. There was a necklace, a pectoral and a multi-tiered tiara. He ran his fingers over the thin metal links that attached the shells. It must have taken ages to create them, and then to find the perfect sized shells and burnish them to an amazing shine.

"Beautiful," he whispered. His grandmother would love this. The workmanship indicated something that should be in a high end jewelry store, if not a museum. "These have got to be one of a kind."

He wondered who had made them. He noticed that the necklace looked rather masculine, yet still had a delicate touch. It was a single fanned shell with a blue cast to one side strung on a thin silver chain. Gabriel found himself stroking his fingers over the silky inside of the shell. He put it around his neck and fastened it.

The cool shell immediately warmed against his skin. He then noticed a thin brown journal lying beneath the jewelry. The leather cover was worn from use. He eased it out of the box and opened it up. The paper inside was yellowed, but still strong. The writing was in a man's hand and quite legible. He started to read an entry near the end.

I know she saw him today. Gabriel blinked. That wasn't really what he had expected to read, but it grabbed his attention. *She was smiling and humming contentedly under her breath. My heart clenched in my chest. How can he—that THING—make her happy when I, her husband, cannot! I swore to myself that I would trust her. But that creature has bewitched her. And there is only one choice left to me now ...*

The writer had pressed down so hard on the paper that it had ripped in places. Gabriel turned to the next page to see what choice the writer meant, but there were no more entries. He quickly flipped back to the first page of the journal. The inner flyleaf had a man's name: Samuel Braven. It was dated from early in the last century.

"An ancestor of ours. Have to ask Grandma about him," Gabriel murmured.

The first entries were more generic with their descriptions of the everyday life of Samuel Braven. He was married to a woman named Tabatha whom he seemed to barely tolerate until she started drawing away from him and towards the "creature." The first entry that indicated something amiss in his marriage was written after Tabatha had gotten caught in a storm and sought shelter in some nearby caves.

She was touching her hair as she told me how she had had to go inside the caves because the downpour was so strong. Lucky for her the tide was not in, otherwise she might have drowned in there. But the caves gave her shelter from the storm. The way she ran her fingers through her long, dark tresses and avoided my eyes as she haltingly told me of this innocent adventure aroused my suspicion that more had happened than what she was saying. But Tabatha has always obeyed me. She knows what she risks if she does not.

A cold chill went through Gabriel. Samuel sounded like a controlling bastard. Gabriel skimmed through a dozen more entries that talked about shipping and local politics. Finally, there was another entry about Tabatha.

She's been going to the caves. Not every day, but enough to make me wonder. Her eyes are bright. There's a lightness to her step. She braids her hair the way she used to for me before we wed and discipline had to be instituted. I followed her yesterday. She was wearing her bathing clothes underneath a loose muslin dress. I thought I was mistaken about her. That she was simply going to swim. But why go so far from the house? Why look so nervous? She kept glancing over her shoulder. It was hard to hide from her gaze. But then I saw them exit the cave together. The man was wearing NOTHING. Even I could see he was perfect. They splashed into the water together and vanished.

Gabriel stared at the page in surprise for a long moment. The darkness of the basement and Samuel's words pressed down on him. He suddenly didn't want to spend another minute in the musty basement that day. He looked at his watch. It was almost four and he hadn't eaten since before eleven. He gathered up the journal along with the jewelry box. He would store it up in his room and look through it later. He would then present it to his grandmother.

She would be thrilled with his find. He took the stairs two at a time.

Chapter 6

CAVE ART

Gabriel stowed the jewelry box in his room before he went in search of Corey. He found his best friend out on the back porch, sprawled in the white string hammock that hung between two of the weathered white columns that held up the roof. Corey had on a pair of dark blue board shorts and a T-shirt that fit snuggly over his protruding belly and biceps. One of Grace's paperback books was loosely held in his large hands. He was deeply engrossed in reading.

"Hard at work, I see," Gabriel said with a good-natured laugh.

"How goes the excavation of the basement?" Corey asked as he stretched his arms over his head and gave a satisfied sigh as his spine popped.

Gabriel swiped at the layer of gray dust that had rained down and collected on the shoulders of his white T-shirt and frowned at the dark streaks that were left behind. "It's going. I swear, why does anyone keep magazines after they've read them? There are like fifty years of *National Geographic* down there."

"Hey! Those are cool, and some are valuable. It's like time travel as you look through them," Corey objected.

Gabriel suddenly noticed that a few of the copies he had brought up from the basement and put in the trash pile had migrated out to the porch and were now lying on the ground beside a perspiring can of Diet Coke.

"I pitched those," Gabriel growled.

"They'll go back in the trash when I'm done with them," Corey promised with a lazy grin.

"Really? They're not going to show up in our apartment next year, right?" Gabriel stared at the magazines with narrowed eyes as if they would suddenly leap up and settle themselves happily on a dusty shelf in his future abode if he didn't.

"Maybe one or two will be important enough—"

"Corey!"

Corey tapped the book against his chin. "Only the most important ones, Gabe! I promise!"

"Hmmmm." Gabriel's eyes narrowed further.

"Maybe you should—uhm, I don't know—have some fun? It might improve your mood," Corey suggested tentatively. "You've been holed up in the dark with the spiders all morning."

"I was thinking of grabbing a sandwich and maybe having a picnic lunch on the beach." Gabriel sighed as he settled down on a piece of old rattan furniture next to Corey. He ran a hand through his black hair. It came back filled with cobwebs and what looked like spider egg sacs. With a grimace of disgust he flapped his hand to get them off.

"Lunch. On the beach. By the water?" Corey clarified.

"Yeah."

"You're making strides, my man!" Corey grinned. "Uhm, I already ate, but I'll come if you want company."

Gabriel laughed. "It's okay. I can see how comfortable you are here. I think I just want to roam around a bit by myself. And that way if I wimp out about the water, I won't have a witness to it."

Corey put the paperback to the side and tented his hands over his mound of a belly. "You're doing really good, Gabe. I'm proud of your progress."

"Are you taking on Freud today in addition to Santa Claus and Cupid?" Gabriel teased. He grew more somber when Corey didn't smile, but instead seemed more concerned. "I'm okay."

"At least you're trying to be," Corey said.

His best friend tipped his head towards the sea. There were two foot waves, bright with foam, crashing against the beach. Gabriel's shoulders twitched. Once again that mixture of sick dread and excitement filled him.

Nothing amazing is coming. Nothing bad will happen. Though that means no one amazing will come, either.

Gabriel stood up. "I'm *going* to be just fine. Maybe Freud suits you the best of all your personas."

"Hell no! I would hate to ask people what they're feeling all the time and then try to figure out how it related to their childhood." Corey mock-shuddered.

"So you do this for me because?"

"Because you're worth it. Besides, Grandma G won't make me more pie if you're a Gloomy Gus all summer," Corey explained.

"Of course, it all comes down to pie," Gabriel laughed.

"Doesn't everything?"

With that Gabriel went into the kitchen, leaving Corey to his reading. He quickly slapped a ham sandwich together. He also grabbed a bottle of soda and another of water. He shoved all of it into his army green knapsack and slid his phone into the front pocket of his shorts. When he walked past Corey on the porch the other boy was already conked out. Soft snores emitted from his mouth. The book he had been reading was splayed flat against his chest.

"Sleep well," Gabriel whispered before he walked down the steps and onto the sand.

The roar of the ocean soon drowned everything else out. His eyes unwillingly drifted towards it. The sea was a deep blue. The waves were topped with pure white foam. The rush and slap of the water against the sand was hypnotic. Gabriel's steps slowed. The ocean was beautiful, but so dangerous. His parents had loved it, and he knew that deep down, he still loved it as well. He could still vividly recall how before their deaths, he would always run into the waves as soon as they came to his grandmother's cottage. The water would glide around his body like silk. He would feel free from gravity's shackles. Back then, he had thought that the best things in life would always be related to the ocean.

Gabriel turned away from the water and began walking. The beach was surprisingly empty. He plopped down on a little hillock of sand. The golden grains were warm against his buttocks and the backs of his thighs. The sun bathed him in clear light. He dug out his sandwich and the bottle of water.

He closed his eyes and looked at the sun through his eyelids. While his eyes were shut, the light turned from golden to red. The sound of the waves washed over him and his heart began to take on the same rhythm as the slap of the water against the hard-packed sand.

When I stepped into the ocean to save those people something happened. Gabriel could almost still feel the *thrum* that had raced outwards into the sea as soon as his skin had touched the water. He grimaced. *I'm making something out of nothing. Romanticizing my life because nothing much happens in it.*

Yet still the feeling of anticipation and sick dread remained. Everything felt suffused by it. He opened his eyes, trying to center himself on land and not in the sea. His gaze slid from the water to the line of cliffs half a mile away. The ground above the beach gradually sloped upwards, rising until it formed a cliff face fifty to seventy feet tall in some places. He squinted and thought he saw several dark openings in the cliff face facing towards the water. Could one of those be the cave that Samuel mentioned in his journal, the one where Tabatha had found her beautiful lover? Gabriel's parents had not allowed him to explore the nearby caves as it was dangerous when the tide came in. Not that Gabriel had ever cared about the caves when there was the sea. His mind drifted back to Samuel and Tabatha.

What decision did Samuel make? Did he kill his wife and her lover? Or did they manage to escape him? I hope they managed to give him the slip and the man died old and alone.

The desire to look inside the cave rose up in him unbidden. He knew that there would probably be no remnants from the affair that had started there nearly a hundred years ago, but it would still give him something to picture as he read the rest of Samuel's journal. It would make the words that much more real, too. Gabriel finished chewing the last bite of his sandwich. He had eaten it without tasting it. He took another swallow of cool water, got up, dusted the sand off his pants and strode towards the caves.

Why am I so excited? It's likely to be just a dank cave. Yet Tabatha and her lover met and spent time together in there. Either their fear of being found out was so great that a mossy cave appealed to them or it's more pleasant inside than I'm imagining.

After several minutes of walking he arrived at the base of the cliff. The rocks around the nearest cave opening had been polished from the constant rush of the ocean. Though the water was still a good distance away from the mouth of this cave now, it clearly flooded the cave at high tide just like Samuel and his parents had warned. He felt a trace of unease imagining being trapped inside when the tide came in, but he was sure he still had time to poke around a bit and get out before he even risked getting his feet wet.

The sand leading into the cave was slightly damp. Inside the air was salty and the sound of the waves took on an almost ghostly echoing quality. With the sun blocked by the solid rock of the cave, a slight chill fell over Gabriel. He rubbed his arms as gooseflesh broke out. He tried to imagine a woman entering here with the roar of a storm above her. She would probably have wanted to stay near the cave's entrance, but the wind would have blown water well inside. She would have been forced to creep further in. Gabriel followed Tabatha's imagined route.

The cave did not go straight into the cliff. Instead there was a slight turn to the right, and then the cave floor began to slope steeply downwards. She probably had gone around this bend to get out of the storm's fury. And then what? Did she see someone? A pale blur in the darkness?

And why was he naked? Or did that only happen the one time that Samuel followed after her?

Gabriel followed the curve of the cave. It went back over one hundred feet before it opened up into a balloon-like pocket at the end. The light coming from the cave opening was all but gone after he had taken just a few steps around the bend. He fished his phone out of his pocket and turned on the flashlight app. The sand beneath his feet was becoming increasingly sodden as he advanced inside the cave. It gave way beneath his feet more than once, and his shoes soon became soaked.

Suddenly his phone revealed a brilliant blue splashed across the side of one of the jutting surfaces on the wall. He reached out and touched it tentatively. An oily powder came off on his hand. Was it chalk or pastels? He wasn't sure. Had some kids come in here and sprayed graffiti everywhere? He played the light further along the wall and gasped. There was a painting, a mural, actually, of life under the sea stretching across the back wall of the cave.

"Beautiful," he whispered. His voice echoed.

The mural's colors were so vivid that they leaped out at him, glowing in the light of his phone. The artist's gift for realism had Gabriel leaning forward, almost touching his nose to the mural itself, as he studied the sea ferns and the fish that darted between them. He swore that the fish he glimpsed in the corner of his eye seemed to flit away from him and hide behind delicate coral fans. Gabriel could almost believe that if he ran his fingers over the side of the fish he would feel scales and not cold stone. He didn't touch anything, though, for fear he would smear and ruin the delicate lines.

Would the oily nature of the chalk keep it from washing away with the tide? But why create art that no one will see anyways?

The mural was mesmerizing. Though Gabriel wasn't an expert, he was sure that the fish depicted on the wall were completely accurate, as were the underwater plants. Whoever had created this piece of art knew the sea like the back of their hand. The unevenness of the wall had been used to full effect to give the painting depth as well. The mural was over twenty feet long. He looked at every inch of the mural, then started over and looked at it again.

I've got to take some pictures, but I can't use the camera without turning off the flashlight.

Gabriel found himself longing to actually see these things underneath the rolling waves. Not just in a dream, but in reality. It had been so long since he had thought of the sea while awake with anything but fear. It was as if a great weight, one he had carried around for years, had been lifted slightly off of his shoulders by seeing such beauty. Looking at the mural, he remembered why he used to love the sea with all his heart and how his subconscious had created that spectacular dream the other night. He wished that he could love it in that uncomplicated a way. He was irritated when the phone's light began to dim. But his irritation fled when he suddenly felt the rush of water over his feet.

The tide!

The water must have been flowing into the cave for some time, but he hadn't noticed. The mural had completely taken over his thoughts. Gabriel flashed the phone over his watch. Somehow he had been in the cave for over an hour. He had completely lost track of time again like he had on the beach the night before. With a curse and a spurt of adrenaline running through his system, he started to head back to the mouth of the cave. But he hadn't gone more than a few steps when his right foot hooked underneath a rock hidden by the water and he fell forward. The phone went flying from his hands and hit the opposite wall. The glow from it went out and darkness flowed over him.

Water and wet sand coated his hands. He pushed himself up to his knees. His heart started hammering against his chest as another rush of water gushed in. The downward slope of the cave was causing the water to come in faster. He feared he didn't have much time before the entire space was submerged.

Don't panic. Just keep ahold of the wall and it'll lead you out. There will be some light to guide you soon. Let your eyes adjust and follow it.

He took in deep breaths. The water was now up to his calves. The smell of salt and seaweed overwhelmed him. The coppery taste of fear coated the back of his tongue.

There's nothing to be afraid of. I've got to keep from panicking. That will get me killed.

He stretched his arms out to the sides. His fingers on one side brushed the rocky wall. He leaned towards it and climbed to his feet. When he had fallen, he had been facing towards the cave's mouth, but now he felt the water pushing at him from behind. He turned towards where the rush of water was coming from.

The water was almost up to his knees now. His khakis were plastered against his legs. The sand kept shifting beneath him, and he felt the current trying to suck his feet out from under him. He stumbled and lost hold of the wall once more. Panicking, his arms flailed wildly and he fell over. The water pushed him back and his head went under the surface.

No!

Gabriel clawed his way out of the water and took in a desperate breath. Why had he ever come in there? Why had he been so foolish as to lose track of time?

Don't think about that. Just get up and move!

The water was now up to his stomach. He could hardly keep his footing. The current was incredibly strong and the water kept rising. He had gone only a few steps before it was up to his chest. His breathing came in panicked gasps. The water kept pushing him towards the back of the cave. For every step forward he managed to take, another wave pushed him three steps back. The water was now up to his neck. He couldn't get any purchase whatsoever on the ground with his feet.

I've got to swim. That's the only way. I'm strong. I can swim my way out of here!

Gabriel toed off his shoes and slipped off his backpack, which had been constraining his arms. He treaded water, feeling lighter without the burden of those things. He started to stroke into the current as it was his only guide now as to which way was out. The darkness in the cave was complete. He realized that the beautiful mural must have been washed away now.

He wasn't sure if he was making any progress. There looked to be no light ahead of him. Just the velvety blackness of the cave. The back of his head struck something. Pain lanced through his skull and his strokes stopped for a moment. He had knocked against part of the cave's ceiling. Full blown panic raced through him. His head was brushing the ceiling! How much air was left?

Another powerful wave thrust him backwards again and his head hit the ceiling even harder than before. His consciousness dimmed as the water flowed over his head and he sank beneath the surface. He tried to push his nose and mouth above the surface of the water. His lips were practically kissing the cold, dark ceiling. He took in one last deep breath before the water reached the top of the cave, filling it completely. There was no more air left.

Chapter 17

THE SILENCE OF DROWNING

abriel knew he had one more shot left at getting out of the cave alive. He had taken his last lungful of air. If he didn't hurry, that might be all he would ever get again. He frantically propelled himself underwater. His arms and legs moved furiously against the strength of the sea. He didn't know if he could hold his breath for over a hundred feet underwater to get to the cave's mouth. He didn't want to consider that no matter what he did it might already be too late. What if he was dead already, but just didn't know it yet?

He brushed his right hand along the wall to guide himself towards the opening of the cave. He thought the cave wall seemed to be curving. If he was at the curve, there was a chance he could get out. But his lungs were already burning, as were his sides. He remembered his sides burning in the same way when he had nearly drowned last time. The skin there felt like it would rip open.

He swam up towards the ceiling as his lungs begged for oxygen. Maybe there was a small air pocket. Desperation had him pressing his lips against the slick rock. He slowly opened his mouth. Water rushed inside. Gabriel gagged, only to take in another mouthful of liquid. His body arched as his lungs strained to find oxygen and found only water.

There was no sound as Gabriel drowned. It was quiet and dark. His sides were on fire. His body spasmed.

I'm dying ... I'm dying ...

He couldn't believe it would end like this. He imagined his grandmother and Corey's pain at his senseless death. If the sea was going to take him, why couldn't it have done so when he was with his parents? Why wait until now?

Suddenly, the skin along his sides felt like it was unzipping in long diagonal stripes. There was a rush of heat, of hot blood-warm liquid, against his inner arms that he imagined really was blood. But instead of pain, Gabriel felt only relief. His body floated in the current, pulled back and thrust forward, almost gently. His lungs no longer hurt.

Why am I not dead? Why am I ... breathing? My God, I'm breathing!

Gabriel didn't move for fear of stopping this miracle. Perhaps if he just stayed still until the tide retreated he would be safe. But that would be hours from now. If this was drowning, he was glad his parents had passed this way. There was no sound. There was no pain. There was just peace as the water rushed all around him. He relaxed. But then he felt something brush his right wrist. He jerked away, but the touch came again. It wasn't a curious fish. Instead, a hand was touching him. For one moment all Gabriel could think of was the dream. The touch felt the same. It was a masculine touch, just like the man's. Logically, he knew it was impossible for it to be the man from his dream, but he found himself calling his rescuer "the man" in his mind anyways. He tried to open his eyes, but they stung from the salt and everything was a blur. Like the lights in the dream had, this time the darkness and the salt were hiding the man from him.

Gabriel linked his fingers with the man's as the man confidently touched him once more. The man began to tow him out of the cave. Realizing that movement wasn't stopping the miraculous fact that he was breathing underwater, Gabriel started to help the man who was helping him. He kicked his feet and stroked with the arm the man wasn't holding. Soon the water ahead of them shifted from black as pitch to gray to clear. Even though his vision was still terribly blurred, he could see shafts of sunlight breaking through the water's surface. He kicked harder.

We're almost out of the cave!

Gabriel blinked furiously underwater. His eyes were stinging from the salt, though, so all he saw of the man assisting him was that he was well-built with long dark hair that waved in the water like a flag flapping in the wind. As soon as they broke free of the cave's walls, Gabriel immediately swam towards the surface. He felt the man try to tug him towards deeper water, but when Gabriel's panicked pulls became apparent the man reluctantly allowed him to head towards shallow water. Gabriel's face finally broke through the surface of the water, and he splashed forward until he was able to stand.

Free! Safe! Yet some part of him rebelled at having gravity reassert itself as he got up on his knees in the surf.

Gabriel tried to take in a deep breath of air even though his body did not feel like it needed it. Immediately, his lungs seized. His body spasmed once more, but this time it was air that was causing him to flail helplessly. He opened his mouth and vomited vast quantities of water. He gasped and choked as water slid back in with every breath he tried to take. His rescuer came up behind him as the waves crashed cruelly against Gabriel's body.

"Be calm. Be serene. Reach for equilibrium," the man said.

"You are not used to the transition yet. Your body will adjust again. Let the water come up. Do not fight it."

The man gently rubbed Gabriel's back until the heaving slowed and stopped. He was able to breathe without gagging. Gabriel nodded his head to indicate to the man that he was all right. Impossibly all right. He started crawling towards dry land. His hands sunk into the wet sand. The waves had turned it into a liquid mush beneath him. The man hesitated in the water, but finally gave in and came after him, helping Gabriel collapse on his front just beyond the rush of the waves. Gabriel turned his head to the side at the last moment to stop himself from breathing in sand. He was shaking so badly he couldn't speak at first. The man again resumed his tender stroking of his back.

"T—thank you," Gabriel managed to get out. His throat hurt and his voice was hoarse.

"There is no need for thanks," the man murmured. His voice really did sound like the man in his dream's. The stroking continued uninterrupted, and soon Gabriel's trembling eased.

"I should be dead," Gabriel said. "I—I thought I was."

"The first transition is a bit like death," the man said. "But I do not understand why you were alone for it. Your fear was like a beacon to me, similar to—it does not matter. I came as fast as I could, but already you were through it. Why was your tranache not with you?"

Transition? Tranache?

"I don't understand what you mean," Gabriel said. He swallowed, trying to get some saliva down his aching throat. "I just went inside the cave to explore and lost track of time when I found this amazing mural, and then the tide came in."

"A mural? That is what kept you in the cave when the tide started coming in?" The man sounded uneasy.

"It was so beautiful that I … well, almost died for it."

"So you did not know, then, that you were transitioning?" The man sounded shocked.

91

"I'm still not understanding what you mean by transitioning." Gabriel lifted himself up and turned to face the man for the first time. The words he was about to say froze in his throat. His tongue stuck to the roof of his mouth as he stared in sudden wonder and surprise.

Beautiful. Stunning. Otherworldly. All of these descriptions popped into his mind. He could not have picked a better person for the man from his dream to be than his rescuer. His rescuer looked to be slightly older than Gabriel. He had long dark hair that was slicked back from his face and hung like a rope of wet silk down his powerful back. His wide eyes were an incredible shade of blue-green and were looking back at Gabriel with confusion. The pupils seemed larger than normal, but it just added to the man's beauty. He had delicately arched eyebrows, a strong jaw and high cheekbones. His lower lip was slightly larger than his upper one, just begging to be sucked on. And that was only his face.

His body was even more incredible. The man's chest was broad and heavily muscled, leading down to a slender waist and muscular thighs. He only wore what looked like a loincloth of shimmering blue-green material that matched his eyes and hung to his knees. The front panel of material had fallen to the side, revealing a long, thick cock. Gabriel flushed hotly and quickly looked away. His own cock, though, twitched in his shorts, and a burst of heat went through him at that simple glimpse. His body was telling him he knew that cock, had been pierced by it to his core. He dragged his eyes back up to the man's face.

His rescuer's eyebrows drew together. He did not open his mouth yet Gabriel clearly heard him ask, *You do not know about the transition? Were you not told of it by your tranache?*

"Your lips aren't moving, but I … I hear you," Gabriel whispered. He touched his temple. "In my mind."

You do not know anything, do you? How could your tranache allow this? It is worse than cruel! Again, the man's lips did not so much as twitch. He gently touched Gabriel's other

92

temple. *I am speaking to you in here. Our minds are one.*

Gabriel let out a shocked laugh. "Telepathic communication? Am I dead? Are you some kind of—of angel or something?"

The word "angel" came out rather strangled. It sounded so trite and ridiculous, but the man was that beautiful. His voice was so calming.

In the dream, he was just like this—NO! That was a dream and this—this cannot be real either!

Gabriel glanced at the hand that still touched his temple. It was then he noticed that there was webbing between the man's fingers. Gabriel jerked away, his eyes going wide. There was a flash of hurt in the man's expression that quickly turned to concern.

"I'm sorry, but ..." Gabriel didn't know what to say. This man was speaking to him with his mind. He had webbing between his fingers. His touch felt the same as the man in his dream's. It was inexplicable. It was impossible.

Like me not drowning. Maybe I hit my head harder than I thought. Maybe this is all a dream. Or a hallucination from lack of oxygen to my brain! But he couldn't convince himself of any of those things. Everything about this moment was as real as anything he had ever experienced.

You do not know what I am. You do not know what you are, the man said telepathically. There was such sadness in his tone, as well as a touch of outrage.

"What *I* am? I'm me—Gabriel. Just me. Nothing—nothing like you. I mean nothing special or ... shit! I'm babbling here. You're talking with your *mind*! How can you do that? How is that possible?" Gabriel asked.

It is the way of the Mer. The man held his hand up and spread his fingers. The webbing went halfway up the man's digits. It was flesh-colored, but laced with bluish veins that shimmered just beneath the skin. Gabriel leaned forward to get a better look. The strange webbing didn't take away from the man's beauty. But it was not like anything Gabriel had ever seen before.

"That's not … normal." Gabriel blanched as soon as he said the word. That had sounded cruel when he had not meant it that way.

But the man didn't seem offended. He merely shook his head sadly. *For humans you are correct.*

He pointed beyond the empty beach towards the far off lights of the town.

"Humans?" Gabriel's voice rose up. "You think I'm not—not … and you're saying that you're also not—not … human?"

I am Mer. You are Mer, the man said.

"A Mer? Wait a minute!" Gabriel let out a slightly hysterical laugh. "That explains it! I'm imagining this. Dreaming again! That's it! It's all because of what Corey, Grandma and I were talking about this morning mixed with the dream I had the other night! That's all. This isn't real!"

It is real. You know it is real. Let us see if you have started to change fully, the man said.

He reached for Gabriel's right hand, easily catching it and drawing it between them. He pulled apart Gabriel's fingers. There was no webbing. Gabriel let out a breath he hadn't known he was holding. For one moment, he had expected the webbing to be there.

"I'm not a Mer! I'm not—not like you," Gabriel said, and he felt a momentary pang of sadness that he was not, but he pushed aside that strange, unnatural wish.

You are becoming like me. This is merely the start. You are older than most. You have avoided the water? the man guessed.

"Uhm, yeah. How did you know that?" Gabriel asked.

The transition would have happened much earlier than this otherwise. You are mostly grown now. The man gestured towards Gabriel's lean form.

Gabriel found himself blushing again. The way the man had said it made Gabriel think he liked what he saw. Gabriel shivered slightly and wrapped his arms around his middle. His wet clothes were now quite cool.

Come. The man extended one hand towards him when he noted Gabriel's shaking. *We should get back into the water. You will be warmer there, and we need to start our journey home soon. You cannot yet go down all the way as you have not fully transitioned, but it will not be long now.*

Gabriel didn't register anything the man was saying other than that he wanted to take Gabriel "home," to a "home" that was clearly not his grandmother's. He realized, too, that this "home" the man wanted to take him to was in the water, *under* the water.

"The water—no! No! NO!" Gabriel yelled the last and retreated from the man a few feet. All his fear of the water slammed back into him. The fact that he had nearly drowned yet again made him more determined than ever to never set foot in the sea again.

The man's eyes widened. *You are frightened of the sea now. I can see it. Your tranache has much to answer for for allowing this all to happen!*

"What is a tranache? I really don't know what you're talking about. I think you're confusing me with someone else."

And I'm confusing you with a man in a dream who would never leave me, Gabriel thought

Gabriel scrambled to his feet. His legs felt like limp noodles beneath him. Gravity seemed to want to crush him. He should leave this strange, beautiful man and get home. Maybe then normality would kick in and this would become a distant, lovely dream. But part of him wanted to stay just to look at the man, even if he wasn't sure that he wanted to hear what he had to say.

Your tranache is the one who gave you your kalish. He pointed to the necklace that Gabriel had taken from the jewelry box in the basement. *Your tranache is responsible for making you.*

Gabriel touched the necklace. The shell's ridges felt smoother than before when wet. "Kalish?"

A symbol of the house you belong to. The man touched the shell. His eyes widened as he took in the delicate ridges of the shell.

No, it cannot be, unless ...

He was so close. Gabriel found himself leaning forward into the man's touch. The man was several inches taller than Gabriel, and though broad shouldered himself, Gabriel was not quite as broad as his rescuer.

He has the same body type as the man I dreamed of. I already know that I would fit perfectly against him, Gabriel realized. But he shook the thought away. This man was mad, or *he* was mad, or Mer, or something.

"No one gave this to me. I found it in my grandmother's basement." Gabriel pointed towards his grandmother's home. He imagined Corey and his grandmother sitting out on the porch, talking and sharing some wine before dinner. He should be back there now. They were probably worried about where he was, worried about him.

The look of consternation passed from the man's features. He whispered, *Braven. It is as I thought.*

"Yeah. I'm a Braven. Gabriel Braven," Gabriel said.

The man nodded. *Now all of this makes sense.*

"Uhm, it does?" Gabriel shifted from foot to foot.

The first generation was not Mer. Nor the second. Nor the third. We believed it had not taken. And after the tragedy, we were not inclined to hurt the Bravens any more, so we stopped watching the successive generations, the man whispered. His brows drew together and he shook his head. *But we were foolish. Liseas is a strong house. We should have known it would come out at some point.*

Gabriel remembered the journal then. The naked man with Tabatha. The one she had found in the cave. Was he a Mer? Had she become pregnant by a Mer?

"This is all crazy. I can't—can't believe what you are saying." Gabriel shook his head violently. He wouldn't believe this nonsense.

You would ignore the fact that you were breathing water as easily as air? the man asked.

"I—that was a fluke. I didn't. I must have ... I don't know!" Gabriel yelled and flapped his hands up and down in consternation.

Will you disbelieve your own eyes, then? the man asked.

"I don't know what you mean. The webbing thing? Some people have that ..." he said uncertainly. "And the telepathic thing ... well, I hit my head pretty damn hard in that cave. Not just once. Twice!"

The man walked to the edge of the water. He bent down and scooped up a handful of the sea. He then turned and walked back over to Gabriel. *Watch.*

He splashed the water down his left side. Gabriel watched in shock as four slits appeared diagonally across his skin.

Gills! Gabriel gasped. He wanted to lean in closer and rear back at the same time.

"Okay. You're a Mer. Impossible as that is. You're a merman!" Gabriel said.

And so are you, the man said.

Gabriel shook his head even as he thought he felt a fluttering at his own sides. He remembered all too clearly the sensation of his skin opening up in the cave and how he could suddenly breathe.

No, that's not possible! I can't believe it's possible! Gabriel thought.

Gabriel, lift your shirt, the Mer said quietly.

"No." Gabriel hugged his arms tightly around him.

Why? the Mer asked gently.

"Because this is ridiculous!" Gabriel said, a hint of panic in his tone.

Because you know what you will see. You are a Mer. You are like me. The man stepped closer to him.

Gabriel swayed towards him as he looked into the man's beautiful eyes. They reminded him of sunlight playing on water. They were mesmerizing. Those strong, powerful arms slowly wrapped around him. He knew this touch. He remembered being held like this. It was even better than in the dream. They fit together

97

like two puzzle pieces. Gabriel found himself laying his head against the Mer's chest. It felt incredible to be embraced like this. For one moment, he felt a connection so strong between them that he wouldn't have been surprised to see a physical cord connecting them.

I know you are afraid, the man said. *But there is no reason to be. You are safe. You will come home now.*

Gabriel stiffened. "I'm not going into the water. I—I can't! I have a home. It's here."

It may be empty, Gabriel thinks. *I may be empty. But it's my emptiness, and at least it's not beneath the sea.*

He struggled against the man's larger form. It was disconcerting to realize that the man was holding him effortlessly. It was only when the man chose to release him that he got a few steps away. Those blue-green eyes regarded him sadly.

Gabriel, you cannot stay on land. The transition has begun. It will not stop. The man caressed Gabriel's cheek. *If you stay here, you will die.*

Gabriel gasped. The man's words seemed to vibrate through him. They had the ring of truth. But staying on dry land meant death? That couldn't be right! Dry land was where he was safe. Dry land was where he wouldn't die. The sea wasn't his home. The sea wanted to take him and drown him. He shook his head.

"I have to go home. I can't do this," Gabriel whispered.

The man lowered his head and shook it. *I see you will not come tonight. I see you will have to be convinced.*

"Nothing you can say can convince me!" Gabriel said with a shudder as he looked at the sea over the man's left shoulder. It seemed more alien and unknowable than ever before now that he knew there were creatures that lived within its vastness that he had thought were only myth.

I will not say anything, Gabriel. Your own body will show you the truth clearer than any words, the man responded.

"We'll see." Gabriel started to turn away from the Mer even

though a large part of him cried out that it didn't want to.

Even though I will physically leave you now, I will still be here. The man touched Gabriel's temple. *When you are ready, we will talk.*

"There's nothing to say."

The man smiled at him. *You know there is. All you need to do is call for me and I will be there.*

"I don't even know your name," Gabriel confessed.

My name is Casillus Nerion.

"Casillus." Gabriel rolled the name over his tongue.

As I said, if you need me, I will always hear your call. Casillus gave him one last caress and then turned and ran into the ocean.

Gabriel watched in admiration as Casillus' strong body cut through the water. He then disappeared beneath the waves. Just as he did, Gabriel thought he heard the same words from his dream, but this time clearly spoken in Casillus' voice.

I will not leave you. I will never leave you.

The Story Continues in Book 2!

The Merman

BOOK 2 - ACCEPTANCE

~A PREVIEW~

Chapter 1

DISBELIEF

Gabriel Braven stared at the spot where Casillus Nerion had disappeared beneath the waves. There was nothing to show that the beautiful man had ever been there, had showed Gabriel impossible things like gills and webbed fingers, had even rescued Gabriel from death in a watery cave in the first place. But the sea was like that. It didn't show anything at all when it had swallowed people up whole. Gabriel had known that all too well ever since his parents' deaths, when their boat had been capsized by a rogue wave when he was just a child. Gabriel had inexplicably survived the sinking. He had vague, dream-like memories of *something* miles high with tentacles taking him back to shore, but he didn't believe they were real memories.

Is Casillus even real or is he like that monster that I dreamed saved me? After all, Casillus said he's a Mer. A real, live merman!

But he also claimed I am, too. That I am "transitioning" or whatever he called it.

Gabriel brought up his right hand before his face and spread his fingers wide. No webbing. He let out a relieved gust of air and dropped his hand back down to his side, but that movement had his wet shirt brushing against his skin, against his sides. Something moved just over his ribs. Something opened and closed, fluttered. Like gills.

No! Gabriel shook his head violently. *I'm not a Mer! I'm human! This is all crazy! Absolutely insane!* But he didn't lift up his shirt to check if there really was something there.

In a daze, Gabriel turned away from the sea and started walking back to his grandmother's house. He knew his grandmother Grace, his best friend Corey Rudman, and Professor Johnson Tims, a professor from Miskatonic University who was running a nearby archeological dig, were all waiting on him for dinner. He had no idea how he was going to be able to act normally around them after this. Because one of two things had happened to him. One possibility was that he had really been saved by a merman and might be a merman himself. Or there was the second possibility, which was that he was really and truly crazy.

Gabriel rubbed his mouth with one hand. The fluttering on his sides continued, but there was no way in Hell he was going to look to see if, like Casillus, he had four slit-like gills on either side of his ribcage. Seeing would be believing and he couldn't believe. He just couldn't.

They shouldn't even be there anatomically speaking! The ribs are like a hard suitcase around the organs. That is the last place gills should be. Wouldn't it make more logical sense if the gills were on my neck?

Gabriel clamped his hand over his mouth to stop hysterical laughter from erupting out of him. His wet shirt stuck to his right side at that moment, and the gills—*no, not gills!*—pushed against the clingy damp material. Gabriel glanced down for a brief second and saw the *rippling* they were causing. He jerked his head up, trying to convince himself that the movement had been caused by an unfelt breeze.

He told himself that the lack of oxygen to his brain from the near drowning had caused him to hallucinate the whole thing. He must have managed to get himself out of the cave somehow and imagined the rest. But Casillus had seemed so real! As real as Corey, his grandmother, or anyone else he had ever met. And Gabriel could still *feel* him out in the water, keeping pace with Gabriel on land. Watching. Waiting.

The dream I had felt real, too, and I know that was just a dream. Yet Casillus' touch was exactly like the man in the dream's.

He had dreamt two nights ago of a lover. A merman lover, if he was being completely honest with himself. He had dreamt of making love underwater to someone that *felt* just like Casillus.

If Corey heard even a sentence of these crazy thoughts he would be saying that this is what happens when someone closes themself off from love: they go crazy!

As his feet pounded against the sand and his grandmother's cottage grew nearer, Gabriel felt the familiar breathlessness he had been experiencing over the past year return and increase.

It didn't use to be "normal." I used to be really fit. But now it's like I'm breathing in molasses. His increased difficulty breathing had to have come from the near drowning. His lungs were strained from that. It had nothing to do with ...

Gabriel, you cannot stay on land. The transition has begun. It will not stop.

... anything like that. Nothing at all. He was a Mer? His family had Mer blood? Ridiculous!

If you stay here, you will die.

And that was even crazier! It was always the *ocean* that had spelled death, not dry *land*. His lungs started to hurt as he made it up the dune that lead to the front of his grandmother's cottage. His sides were throbbing. Every time his wet shirt brushed against them they burned, as if something—*the gills, no, not gills!*—was being irritated by the constant shift of material over them. He slowed to a walk and then a crawl as he climbed up the stairs to the front porch.

He leaned on the porch's railing, bending over it as he took in deep breaths, but he still wasn't getting in enough air. His lungs felt like they were filled with sand. Hands shaking, he placed his palms over where the gills would be if such things were real. He felt something move beneath them. He jerked his hands away. His own body was alien to him all of the sudden. He covered his face with his hands.

Am I crazy? Is it possible for crazy to feel this real?

"Gabriel?" His grandmother's voice came from inside through the screen door. A warm light shone down the hallway from the kitchen. "Is that you, sweetie?"

"Uh, yeah, Grandma." Gabriel brought his hands down from his face even as sweat suddenly started peppering his upper lip and forehead. Panic fluttered in his chest. His grandmother couldn't see him like this. He was wet. He was sandy. He might have gills! No, he couldn't have gills. He couldn't! But just being wet and sandy alone would raise questions about him getting into the water that he didn't want to answer, that he simply *couldn't* answer.

"Well, what are you doing out there? Come on in! Johnson will be here any moment," she called out gaily.

He could smell steaks sizzling. The sound of his grandmother chopping something, maybe onions and tomatoes to be roasted, and the quieter shush of the waves washed over him.

"Yeah, Gabe, grab a brew and come sit down with us!" Corey called out as well.

"Y—yeah. In a minute. I'm all … uh, sweaty. I'm just going to grab a quick shower and I'll be right down." Gabriel darted inside and then ran directly up the stairs to the bathroom.

He shut the door tightly behind him and sagged against the wall opposite the sink. The lights were off, but even in the windowless room he could see a bare outline of himself in the mirror from the light that streamed through the crack under the bottom of the door. His left hand slowly moved up to the light switch.

Just turn it on. I can't keep standing here in the dark. What am I afraid of? A mirror? Myself? Gabriel swallowed. He could still feel the phantom press of whatever it was on his sides against his palms. He shook his head. *I don't have to look at myself at all. Not that there will be anything to see. I'll throw off my clothes and get in the shower. Wash off the salt. Then get dry. Everything will be fine.*

But he still hesitated to switch on the light. His breath came in harsh gasps.

I still don't feel like I'm getting enough air.

A cry started to slip out of his mouth, but he immediately slammed a hand over his lips to hold it in.

Nothing's wrong. Nothing at all. Just switch on the light. Don't look in the mirror.

He flipped on the light, but he didn't honor his promise not to look in the mirror. He couldn't help himself. He couldn't look away. He had to see. He wasn't sure what he expected—or feared—to see. But when he saw his eyes looking back at him in the stark glass, all hopes that he would look no different after his experiences that day were lost. He stumbled over to the sink. His eyes looked *wrong*. His eyes looked like Casillus' had: an iris larger than a human's with a pupil that was far more dilated, leaving only a slender ring of color around the edge. He held his right eye open further and just stared.

Not normal. Not human.

"Oh, my God, what am I going to do?" Gabriel whispered.

There was a knock at the door. Gabriel jumped and clutched at the sink. His heart hammered in his chest and it took him a moment to catch his very shallow breath.

"Hey, Gabe, are you okay?" Corey asked.

"Yeah, yeah, I'm fine." But Gabriel knew that he didn't sound fine. Instead, his voice was high and brittle.

"Really?" Corey sounded about as convinced as Gabriel felt. "I can tell something is up with you. Seriously, open the door. You can't hide from me in there."

"I'm—I'm showering, Corey," Gabriel said.

"Since when are you shy?" Corey asked.

He wasn't. Living in tight quarters in the dorm room hadn't allowed for real privacy, not that he was particularly modest in any event. But the changes to his eyes made seeing Corey at that moment impossible. If Corey saw him and noticed something wrong then this would all be real. And it simply could not be real. Gabriel would not allow it.

"It sounds like you're actually curious to see me this time." Gabriel gave out a shaky laugh.

"You're cute, don't get me wrong, but I like the curvier variety of human," Corey retorted.

Gabriel closed his eyes. *Human? No, Corey, I'm not even that.*

"I just wanted to hand you this extra beer I picked up," Corey said. "But if you don't have any need for it, I'll just drink it myself."

Alcohol sounded perfect right then. "Give it here."

Gabriel cracked open the door and Corey stuck one of his pudgy arms in. There was an ice cold Corona in his hand. Gabriel grabbed it and took a deep swallow. He let out a groan of pleasure. His throat suddenly wasn't as tight as the alcohol flowed down. He rested the cold bottle against his hot forehead.

"So are you really okay?" Corey asked. "You sound a little … *off.*"

"I'm—I'm good." Gabriel laid his forehead against the door as he quietly shook.

"Did something happen on the beach? You didn't try to go into the water again, did you? Save another drowning person?"

Gabriel stifled another inappropriate laugh. *Another drowning person? This time it was me.*

"I didn't save anyone today," Gabriel said faintly. *Casillus did.*

"I think there's a rule that you can only save two people a week," Corey chuckled. There was a slight pause before he said in a more serious tone, "If you're suddenly … ah, *not* good, I'm here, you know?"

Gabriel swallowed, realizing that his best friend thought his odd behavior came from being upset about his parents. "Y—yeah, I know. That means a lot, Corey."

"Well, anything I can do, man. Seriously. I can only imagine how hard it is being back here and stuff. You're being a real trooper."

Gabriel just nodded even though Corey couldn't see him. His throat had closed up. He felt sick for lying. *I can't show Corey this. I can't show anyone!*

"I'll be downstairs in a second, Corey. Leave me some steak," Gabriel said weakly.

"No problem!"

Gabriel's heart hurt as he listened to Corey pad away. He ripped off his clothes and turned on the shower. He was sticky with salt. He wanted to wash that off at least. Then he froze, half-in, half-out of the water.

Should I risk getting even wetter? The gills might stay longer. The gills …

Gabriel threw himself into the shower, determined not to continue that thought and even more determined not to consider it further. His skin had been feeling increasingly tight and dry, but as soon as water poured over his body the tightness went away. He let out a sigh and allowed his head to tilt back into the spray. His eyelids slid closed. At first the normal darkness appeared behind his eyelids, but suddenly he thought he saw a flash of light. His forehead furrowed. He opened his eyes to see what it was and the cream tiled wall swam before his vision. The light from the wall sconces above the sink was a steady glow.

Must have been nothing.

He relished the warm stream of water running down his face, throat, chest, and stomach, trickling down the length of his cock. The pleasant heat relaxed his muscles and his lungs. But still he was careful not to let his arms brush his sides.

His eyes slid closed again, and this time instead of the normal black tinged with red he saw a murky blue, like moonlight streaming through water. His breath froze. He was definitely "seeing" something. There were motes drifting through patches of moonlight and down towards the sea floor far below him. He felt his head turn and saw a distant light from shore. How he knew that way was towards shore was a mystery to him, but he was sure it was.

Those are the lights from Grandma's house.

Gabriel? Casillus' warm voice asked. *Are you with me?*

Gabriel's eyelids flew open. He stumbled forward as the world seemed to spin and reform back into the bathroom shower. He caught himself from falling forward onto his face just in time by throwing out one hand towards the wall.

What the hell is happening to me?

He turned off the water and staggered out of the tub. He toweled off quickly, continuing to be careful not to let his palms touch the skin along his sides. But even so he felt a fluttering, felt the skin moving where it shouldn't. Panic rippled through him. He gathered up his clothes and raced across the hallway into his bedroom and quickly shut the door behind him. He could already hear voices and laughter from down below.

I just need to be with people. All of this—this weirdness— will stop if I'm not by myself.

He pulled on the first random clothes that he found in his suitcase as he hadn't unpacked yet. He had a feeling he was wearing all mismatched things, which would make him look more like Corey than like his more conservatively dressing self, but he didn't care. He just wanted everything to be covered. Especially his sides. He refused to look down at his chest at all. As soon as he had a shirt on, some of the tension bled out of his body. He sank down on his bed for a minute, trying to compose himself. He had to act normally once he made it downstairs.

Can I do that?

He let out a soft laugh and ran his fingers through his damp locks, arranging them. He felt the kalish shift against the hollow of his throat. His fingers skimmed over the top of it. The shell was cool and smooth under his fingertips. He slipped the kalish beneath his T-shirt at the same time as his gaze fell on the jewelry box he had found in the basement. The box was on the floor tucked up against the wall opposite him. He stilled.

Samuel Braven called his wife's lover a "thing." A "creature." He also described him as naked, kind of like Casillus was. A scrap of cloth wrapped around his hips hardly qualifies as clothes.

Gabriel slid off the bed and onto his knees in front of the box. His right hand hesitated over the lid. The journal was inside. He could show it to his grandmother. Maybe it would jog her memory. She would be able to tell him that Tabatha's lover was a local fisherman or something. Not a Mer.

Gabriel, can you hear me? Casillus' voice ghosted through his mind again. It was faint. *Are you all right? I sense such fear and confusion in you. There is no need for either. Come to me now and I can assist you.*

Gabriel ignored the voice even though it was kind and warm and a part of him wanted to respond back to it. But he wouldn't! Because that voice would drag him over into insanity, or further into insanity. He wasn't sure anymore which it was. He would have to believe impossible things, and he just couldn't do it. For a moment, he thought of the unnamed protagonist of his own story, who had sacrificed his mind, and then his life, to love a Mer. Was he having some kind of bizarre break with reality like his character had had?

But the gills on my sides are real ... NO! There are no gills! There are no mermen! I refuse to believe!

Shaking, Gabriel decided the best way to block out this

110

craziness was to join the others in the dining room. He yanked open the jewelry box and grabbed the journal. He would show it to his grandmother. Gabriel got off his knees and hustled downstairs, determined to forget everything that had happened that day in the sea.

If you enjoyed *The Merman – Book 1: Transformation*, check out another title by X. Aratare, *The Artifact – Book 1: The Bodyguard*.

Sean Harding is a born protector. As a police detective for the wealthy city of Winter Haven, Sean thinks he has found his purpose, but then things go terribly wrong and he loses his partner, his job and even hope. That is until he meets Dane Gareis …

Dane Gareis is a wealthy, reclusive young man with a traumatic past, but a spine of steel. When his father is killed in a mysterious plane crash, Dane carries on the family business and continues his passion for the very antiquity that got his father murdered — a golden sarcophagus belonging to an ancient cult known as the Ydrath.

Soon, the Ydrath threaten him as well, and Dane seeks to hire a bodyguard he can trust. Someone who can protect him, and someone who will respect his boundaries. While he gets the first two, the third requirement falls apart when he hires Sean Harding.

Sparks immediately fly between them. And as it turns out, there is more to connect them than simply a job.

Read the preview of chapter one...

THE ARTIFACT – Book1: The Bodyguard

CHAPTER 1
SOLE SURVIVOR

Detective Sean Harding thrust open Winter Haven Memorial's emergency room doors. He strode past the nurse on duty with a flash of his detective badge and a curt nod. The badge was a necessity. As an undercover operative for the Winter Haven Special Task Force and Narcotics Unit, known simply as "the Unit," he didn't look the part of a police detective even when he wore a suit like today.

His dark brown hair was long enough for it to begin to curl and brush the tops of his shoulders, and he had a perpetual five o'clock shadow. His olive-toned skin spared him from looking vampire-pale despite long hours spent on night-darkened streets and in the windowless rooms of clubs. But despite having been up for over thirty-six hours straight, Sean's green eyes still looked sharp and clear.

He hadn't stopped moving since first hearing about the drug that was known simply as the Powder. Everything surrounding the drug was shrouded in darkness. Where it came from, who was behind its manufacture, and even its actual chemical makeup were all unknown. The only thing that was certain was that it killed everyone who took it. And that fact made Sean fear there would be a holocaust of drug users unless he could locate the source of the Powder and choke off its flow. He had finally gotten his first solid lead tonight in the form of a phone call from Dr. Olga Vostok, a good friend and emergency room physician at Winter Haven Memorial.

"Sean," Dr. Vostok had said. "We have a survivor."

"Are you sure?" His heart rate had risen.

"Yes. He's a young man. More like a boy. He took the Powder and he's here. Alive," she had said, her voice rushed and strained.

"Keep him alive, Olga. If he says anything—I mean ANYTHING, write it down, record it, remember it. Do whatever you have to do," Sean had ordered. As soon as he had hung up, he had jumped into his car, peeled out of the police station's parking lot. He got to the ER in record time.

And now he was here, in the hospital, feet away from the boy that could turn his investigation around. Sean yanked aside the curtain that surrounded the boy's hospital bed. The sound of the metal rings sliding along the pole was nearly deafening. He froze.

Too late.

Sean recognized death when he saw it. His gaze riveted on the red blood oozing out of the corners of the boy's unseeing blue eyes. It looked especially vibrant against the child's chalky white skin. The blood trails were dry, appearing almost painted on in their vividness. For a moment, Sean wanted to grab the boy's shoulders and shake him. He wanted to believe that the red was makeup or paint. But he knew it was not. The boy was dead and gone. Sean swallowed the bile that rose in his throat.

"His brain liquefied. We will need an autopsy to confirm it, but I am sure already. Just like the others," Dr. Vostok's Russian-accented voice suddenly came from behind him. Startled, Sean spun around to face her. His first thought was that she looked as deathly pale as the boy. "Sorry. Didn't mean to scare you, Sean."

Sean waved off her apology even as his heart still thundered in his chest. "How long ago did he die?"

"Moments after I called you, so the guilt in your eyes is unfounded. You couldn't have gotten here in time unless you had teleported." She touched his shoulder tenderly, but he didn't want tenderness. The disappointment was too great.

"He is—*was*—the only lead I had, Olga. More are going to die, because I didn't get here fast enough."

Dr. Vostok walked over to the boy's bed. Her dark blonde hair gleamed under the fluorescent lights. The lines that framed her mouth deepened as she looked down at the dead boy. She lightly placed one of her hands on the child's forearm. Sean noticed that her nails were bitten to the quick.

"He took the Powder just once," she said softly. "Just once, and this was the result. He looks all of fifteen, doesn't he?"

"Any ID?" Sean's police instincts kicked in even as his shoulders slumped in exhaustion and despair. Another lead to nowhere.

"No, no ID. No wallet. He didn't even have on shoes or a shirt when he wandered into the ER," she said, patting the boy's arm.

"Did he say who he bought the drug from?" Sean asked.

She shook her head. "He would only speak of what the drug showed him."

116

"So it causes hallucinations?" Sean asked wearily. He expected a quick confirmation from Dr. Vostok, but she was silent for so long that Sean began to feel a trickle of unease. "Olga?"

"I don't know," she said, then shook herself. "I mean, most probably. Yes, definitely, it causes hallucinations. He couldn't have really been seeing what he claimed he was. It's quite impossible." The last was said softly, almost as if she were speaking to herself.

Sean grasped her elbow gently. "What is it? You look unnerved. I've never seen you like this."

"Unnerved? That's a very good word to use to describe how I feel." She wrapped her arms around herself as she added, "This drug, Sean, it isn't like anything I've ever seen. If you had heard what he *said*. His voice is still in my mind."

"Tell me," Sean urged.

"He said that I should think of reality as a matryoshka," she said.

"A matryoshka?" Sean asked. The word was alien on his tongue, and didn't sound like something a fifteen-year-old would know.

"It is the Russian term for a traditional Russian nesting doll," she explained. "You know, the wooden dolls where, when you open them, there are other dolls inside."

"Oh, I've seen those." Sean's brow furrowed as his confusion grew with the explanation. "And he used the word 'matryoshka'?"

"Yes, it is strange, isn't it?" Dr. Vostok let out a soft, uneasy laugh. "And what's even stranger is that I believe he used that metaphor just for *me*. Just so that *I* would understand. But if he had been speaking to someone else, he would have used a different metaphor. A metaphor that would have resonated for that person." She wrapped her arms around herself again. "He was dying, Sean. His brain was literally becoming soup in his skull, but he was thinking at such a level—I cannot explain it."

"Did he say anything else about this—this nesting doll metaphor?"

She nodded. "He said that I should imagine that the outermost nesting doll is the world as we know it. That doll is the reality we can see. But the drug, the Powder, has the ability to pull that doll apart and show us what is inside."

"And what does the inside look like?" Sean asked, that earlier trickle of unease becoming a torrent.

"Beautiful and terrible." Dr. Vostok shivered. "He told me that just one layer down from here, just *one*, things get a whole lot more interesting, but if you continue on, you will find ..." She suddenly stopped and let out a nervous little laugh that had the hair on the back of Sean's neck standing on end.

"What do you find?" Sean asked, resisting the urge to shake her. His desperation to know *anything* about the drug rose up in him stronger than ever.

Her eyes were bright, glassy with unspeakable unease, as she said, "You'll find that we're not alone. But having seen who we're sharing all of this with, you'll wish we were."

*****

The full book is available in our shop in ePub, Kindle, PDF, paperback and there is also an audio-book version on Amazon, Audible and iTunes!

PUBLISHING

<u>Raythe Reign Deals & Coupons</u>

Are you in the mood for more dark, sexy m/m stories? Check out our online shop here, where you can find ALL available works from us (some not available on Amazon.)

http://shop.raythereign.com

And if you want to be the first to know about new Raythe Reign releases, join our update list!

We'll send you a note as soon as the next volume is out. People on our update list will also get some insider info...

- <u>Exclusive monthly deals</u> for books and manga through our own shop.
- Coupons for our monthly membership, which has *something new to see or read* every day of the year (even Christmas!)
- Contests, giveaways, and things like AMAs (ask-me-anything sessions.)
- Events we're participating in, such as conventions, discussion panels, etc.
- Progress updates about current series, new series, stories, and side content.

- Exclusive content you can ONLY find through our shop, such as sexy stories and graphic novels that are <u>too hot for Amazon</u> to sell.

Join here: <u>http://shop.raythereign.com/raythe-reign-update-list/</u>

- Raythe Reign Team

Made in the USA
Middletown, DE
30 September 2015